"A Horse
Just Like

"All this running around he's doing—it's a search."

Dash watched her as she stared back at the untamed colt. Two wild and beautiful creatures. Puzzled but intrigued, he found himself believing Molly Pym.

"All right," he said. "Will you work with him?"

Molly straightened up and looked at Dash squarely. "Yes, I'll work with him," she said. "But not with you."

"We come as a set, I'm afraid."

"It's a set we'll have to break."

Dash shook his head. "No deal."

Molly's face filled with a desperate eagerness. "But I can *help* him! I can make him feel better, settle him down. I'll take him to my place and—"

"No, I want you here. Both of you."

"But—"

"It's not negotiable. You've got us both, Miss Molly, or neither one."

Dear Reader:

Welcome to Silhouette Desire – provocative, compelling, contemporary love stories written by and for today's woman. These are stories to treasure.

Each and every Silhouette Desire is a wonderful romance in which the emotional and the sensual go hand in hand. When you open a Desire, you enter a whole new world – a world that has, naturally, a perfect hero just waiting to whisk you away! A Silhouette Desire can be light-hearted or serious, but it will always be satisfying.

We hope you enjoy this Desire today – and will go on to enjoy many more.

Please write to us:

Jane Nicholls
Silhouette Books
PO Box 236
Thornton Road
Croydon
Surrey
CR9 3RU

NANCY MARTIN

GOOD GOLLY, MISS MOLLY

Silhouette Desire

Originally Published by Silhouette Books
a division of
Harlequin Enterprises Ltd.

*First published in Great Britain in 1993
by Silhouette Books, Eton House, 18-24 Paradise Road,
Richmond, Surrey TW9 1SR*

© Nancy Martin 1993

*Silhouette, Silhouette Desire and Colophon are
Trade Marks of Harlequin Enterprises B.V.*

ISBN 0 373 58990 5

22-9309

Made and printed in Great Britain

NANCY MARTIN

has lived in a succession of small towns in Pennsylvania, though she loves to travel to find locations for romance in larger cities—in this country and abroad. Now she lives with her husband and two daughters in a house they've restored and are constantly tinkering with.

If Nancy's not sitting at her word processor with a stack of records on the stereo, you might find her cavorting with her children, skiing with her husband or relaxing by the pool.

Other Silhouette Books by Nancy Martin

Silhouette Desire

Hit Man
A Living Legend
Showdown
Ready, Willing and Abel
Looking for Trouble

One

Dash O'Donnelly braked his English sports car to a neck-snapping stop just in time to avoid crashing through the gate that stood between Dash and the one woman who could save his life.

A hand-lettered sign hung crookedly on the gate: Keep Out. Trespassers Will Be Shot.

A sign wasn't going to stop Dash, though. Pym Stables had been one of the most respected racing stables in the Saratoga area. But now Paddy Pym was dead and his reclusive daughter, Molly, lived alone at the farm. Judging by her sign, she didn't care to do business anymore.

But things were going to change, whether she liked it or not.

Dash glowered at the sign and muttered, "Everything I've heard about you better be true, Miss Molly. Because you're my last option."

The overgrown bushes were too close to open the car door, so Dash climbed out of the convertible. He cursed as he pressed bare-handed through the thorny brambles surrounding the car. By way of reprimand for his language, a blackberry bush lashed out and slapped him across the face.

Automatically Dash swiped his palm down his cheek and glared at the trickle of scarlet on his hand. "Drawing blood already, I see. Well, two can play that game, Miss Molly."

He waded through the rest of the underbrush and cleared the old gate in a single vault. On foot, he set off up the winding lane.

The June air was still full of morning dew and the scent of lilacs, which any other kind of man might stop to enjoy for a moment. But not Dash. Not today. He marched up the lane without looking right or left at the unmistakable signs of carefully planned gardens run wild. Long-ignored roses climbed rampantly over the broken fence and up along the hanging branches of the oak trees—their blossoms ready to burst open as soon as the afternoon turned hot. Clumps of forsythia and sweet william grew unchecked through the wispy grass and mountains of weeds.

Beyond the weed-ridden fence lay pasture. The fields were shaded by old trees and grew lush with the kind of upstate New York grasses that made for first-rate grazing. Once, those pastures had been full of hot-blooded Thoroughbreds that raced all over the rest of America.

But not anymore.

At the curve of the lane, Dash spotted the first sign of human habitation. A quaint but aging Victorian house stood to the left of the road, rising from an enormous growth of untamed shrubbery. The veranda sagged dangerously, and the turret cried for a new coat of paint.

The house wasn't important, though. The farm's value lay in its land, its history and its heart. Its magic.

Dash could only hope those things still existed.

"Hello!" he called in the direction of the house. "Where the hell is everybody?"

No answer.

He headed for the barn, located just two-dozen steps from the front porch. Dash found himself in a cobblestone yard that could have come straight out of an Irish picture book. But like the house, the barn was very old and showing signs of age. The stone foundation had begun to crumble, and the jaunty red paint on the window trim had blistered and peeled—a far cry from the opulent stables of more successful operations.

A throaty bark suddenly erupted from inside the barn.

A second later, an enormous dog burst from the shadows of the open door—the ugliest dog Dash had ever seen. It hurtled toward him as if closing in on his last meal.

"Hell's fire!"

Dash had just enough time to leap a water trough and scramble up a gnarled apple tree before the mangy hound threw himself at Dash's trouser leg and came away with a mouthful of twill and argyle.

Dash clutched a tree branch and dangled in midair. "You ugly mutt! That was a brand new sock!"

The old hound dropped his mouthful, then sat down happily and commenced to pant—his long red tongue hanging out and his big, floppy mouth curved

in a satisfied canine smile. He was incredibly ugly—
part bloodhound and part every other breed known to
man—with a rough brown coat speckled with black
spots and a face whitened with age. He had one blue
eye and one brown, and—Dash noted at last—only
three legs. His left hind appendage was completely
missing, although the dog didn't seem to mind a bit.

Dash wrapped both arms and one leg around the
tree branch and heard it give a moan of distress beneath his weight. To the dog, he snapped, "Go away,
damn you!"

The dog woofed and gave no sign of moving.

"Clear out!" Dash glared down at the beast from
his unsteady perch. "Don't you know a paying customer when you see one?"

"He knows a trespasser when he sees one," countered a female voice from the depths of the barn.
"And he sure hasn't taken a shine to you, has he,
pretty boy?"

Dash squinted through the apple blossoms at the
woman who stepped into the sunlight.

Dash didn't know what to expect. From all the wild
rumors he'd heard, Molly Pym might have been one
of those motherly farm types with a bosom like the
prow of the *Queen Mary* and hands big enough to
shoe a Clydesdale without any trouble. Or maybe she
was a rail-thin crone who took the appearance of her
horses more seriously than her own.

Dash did *not* expect her to be a knockout.

He nearly fell from his branch as she stepped
through the door and into the yard. She was slender
and tawny, languidly leaning one shoulder against the
door as she continued to wind a lunge line around her
arm. Her brilliant russet hair was caught up on the

crown of her head in some kind of topknot that had started to fall apart, sending brilliant wisps to frame her narrow, suntanned face. A faded checkered shirt clung deliciously to her breasts before disappearing into a pair of soft jeans that hugged her hips with the familiarity that comes from daily wear. She looked lithe and sexy—the kind of woman who ought to be kidnapped for a reason very different from the one Dash had in mind.

Just then Dash's branch gave another moan of distress, yanking his mind off capturing beautiful women. "No wonder this place is such a wreck," he cracked. "Do you chase off every prospective client before he gets a chance to state his business?"

"Prospective client?" She tossed the lunge line onto a nearby bale of straw and sauntered out of the shadows. "Is that what you are, pretty boy?"

Dash held on tight and gritted his teeth. "I've come to talk business. Let me down from here and—"

"I like you better right where you are." She squinted up at him suspiciously. "I bet you're one of those guys from the bank, aren't you? Trying to sneak in here to repossess things while my back is turned."

Dash hung grimly on to the tree limb, trying not to look ridiculous and getting madder by the moment. "I'm not from the bank."

"Oh, yes, you are." She folded her arms over her chest and said, "You're one of those fellows who talks sweet on the phone, then comes out here to hassle me when my payments are five minutes late, right?"

"Wrong!"

She laughed, her face winsome, young and full of sparkle. "I think you're lying to me, pretty boy."

"I am *not* from a bank, and I'm no 'pretty boy,' either. Just let me down and I'll explain everything!"

"Anybody who comes to a farm wearing shoes like yours and—hell, those are actually suspenders under that cashmere jacket, aren't they? What went wrong? Did you leave your straw boater at the country club?"

With his branch bending ominously groundward, Dash said, "I have to put in an appearance at an important luncheon today, as a matter of fact—"

"Luncheon," she said with a derisive hoot. She addressed the dog. "Did you hear that, Seabiscuit? He's going to a *luncheon.*"

The ugly hound gave an appreciative bark that sounded very much like a laugh.

"Look here, smart ass," Dash snapped, "I don't know what kind of problems you've got with the bank, but I can assure you there are a few basic lessons in business that would do you a lot of good."

Her eyes were gleaming with merriment. "You think so?"

"Yes. Like treating people with respect, for starters."

"That sounds a lot like bootlicking to me."

"You could answer your phone once in a while!"

"There's nobody I want to talk to."

"Nobody?"

"Not a soul," she said with a proud lift of her pointed nose.

"Well, that," Dash said in a different tone, "is a shame."

She reacted at once, turning cold and haughty. "Look, pretty boy, you can't come waltzing in here—"

"Who's waltzing? I'm barely hanging on for dear life. Now, call off your dog and let me down before I decide to take my money elsewhere. Or aren't you interested in money?"

"I don't need it."

"Oh, I can see that. This place looks extremely prosperous at the moment. I especially like the jungle you've planted on the other side of that fence."

"You calling my farm a dump?"

"Certainly not. I *like* weeds myself. And the barn looks great. But has the fire marshal been here lately?"

"Just who the hell are you, anyway?"

"I told you before. A prospective client."

She glared up at him for half a minute, clearly weighing her options. Dash glared back.

"All right, Biscuit," she said at last. "Back off."

At once the beast flopped in the dust, closed his eyes and heaved a sigh of complete relaxation like an old man stretching out on a sunny beach.

Just in time. With a snap, Dash's branch gave way. Only a gymnastic midair twist saved him from thudding on his head smack-dab in front of the sexy young woman in blue jeans.

Instead, he managed a relatively dignified, albeit breathless landing on both feet. Straightening, he dusted off his trousers and glowered at Molly Pym as if to dare her to crack a smile.

She didn't. But Dash suddenly decided she had the most astonishing blue eyes—the kind of long-lashed Irish eyes perfect for gazing into over a bottle of champagne. Or after a long night of lovemaking when they'd be smoky with sexual exhaustion. The rest of her wasn't quite so romantic, however. Her hands were rough, the nails short and split. Her sharp-chinned face was quite tan, sprinkled with freckles and un-adorned by makeup. Her clothes were so worn that Dash wondered if the shirt might have been her father's long ago. The boots on her feet had seen better days, too, and the faintest scent of hay-filled barns clung to her body.

But what a body. Dash couldn't help but admire her lean curves, the hint of pert breasts, the legs as long as a dancer's. It all added up to a very enticing woman. He could almost feel those long legs around him and see that mass of long red hair spread out over a pillow.

The fire that burned in her eyes, however, demanded respect.

Deciding he'd better play it safe for the moment, Dash reached out his hand and said, "I think we got off on the wrong foot."

"We're not on any foot at the moment," she retorted, ignoring his offered handshake. "Why don't you just tell me who you are and what you want."

"All right. I presume you're Molly Pym?"

She folded her arms across her chest again and eyed him askance. "And if I am?"

"Do you still train horses?"

"Sure."

"When you get the chance, of course."

Her gaze sparked again. "What's that supposed to mean?"

"Don't get your dander up. Are you fully booked at the moment?"

"What's it to you?"

"My dear girl—"

"I'm not your *girl* or anybody else's," she exploded. "So unless you've got something important to say—"

"Simmer down. I simply want to know if you have time to work for me."

She laughed then, glancing down at his fine clothes. "Doing what? Training ponies for your spoiled children?"

He held on to his temper. "No, training a racehorse. A good one."

She narrowed her gaze. "I don't train racehorses for just anyone."

"I get the impression you aren't training at all just now."

"I keep busy."

Dash couldn't stop a laugh. "Yes, chasing off bankers. That must keep you plenty busy."

She stepped forward and jammed one finger into his chest. "Listen, pretty boy, I've got work to do. Unless you can come to the point within thirty seconds, I'm going to—"

"I have a problem horse. He's good, but he's wild."

That was enough to grab her interest. She stepped back and gave Dash her full attention.

He spoke fast to keep her on the hook. "I've got a colt we can't control at all. None of my people can even get a saddle on him."

"Sometimes you just have to give up trying to race a wild animal. Let him grow up awhile."

"I can't do that. This colt is special. He's going to be great—maybe the greatest colt in twenty years. We've got to get him on the track." Dash didn't want to explain his reasons. "But this animal's crazy. Completely loco."

"Did you cut him?"

Dash shook his head. "I don't want a gelding. I need a colt who can stand at stud once he's done racing." He refrained from explaining just how badly he needed a quality stallion just now and said, "His bloodlines are—well, something I don't want to let go."

"Repeat the breeding. If this one's so much trouble, try again."

"I can't," said Dash. "His sire was Scalloped."

Molly Pym understood. Scalloped was one of the greatest horses in racing history. An animal with more speed, heart and stamina than any of his contemporaries. But he was dead, and everyone in racing had mourned his passing last year.

Molly Pym smiled wryly. "Scalloped was a miracle. But none of his colts were worth the hay to feed them."

Dash tried not to wince. The truth hurt. "This one's different," he said.

"How do you know?"

"If you take one look at him, you'll see what I mean. He's the one."

By watching her face, Dash saw she was interested. Scalloped had been an amazing racer, but an unspectacular father. The fact that he hadn't been able to produce a single winner had been a source of gossip and speculation throughout the entire industry. The odds alone assured at least one promising result from years of Scalloped standing at stud. Dash knew he finally had a colt that would redeem Scalloped's reputation. In his heart, he felt the colt was going to write a new page in the history books.

Molly tilted her head in a flounce of red hair and looked at Dash skeptically. "Where do I come in?"

"I'm told you're good. The best, in fact, with trouble horses."

"Who told you that?"

He shrugged. "People. Blackie Singleton. George Clark. Monty Roy. And others."

The names Dash reeled off were old codgers, all friends of Paddy Pym, Molly's famous but deceased father. "George claims he put you on your first pony. You weren't quite two years old yet. And Monty remembers you finishing a session with a rambunctious filly—after she'd broken your arm in two places. Blackie even said he used to change your diapers."

Flushing a little, Molly said gruffly, "Maybe I ought to sue you for invading my privacy."

"No need for that. All the old-timers love you. They respect you. They told me you're the best, and I want to hire you."

She smiled coolly at Dash. "I guess somebody should have mentioned my methods."

"I've heard you're unorthodox."

She laughed at his choice of words. "Yeah, 'unorthodox,' all right. I've been banned from a half-a-dozen tracks, you know."

"Unofficially."

"Most people think I'm crazy."

"But your methods work."

"How do you know?"

He shrugged. "I visited Mirabelle. And I saw the videotapes."

He shook her up with that, Dash could see. She frowned and said, "Those tapes were supposed to be destroyed."

"They weren't. I've seen what you can do."

"Do you believe I can really do it?"

For a second Dash didn't answer. Of course nobody really believed she could tame a wild horse in a matter of seconds. But Mirabelle had been a hopeless case until Molly Pym had worked her charms. Dash had seen the proof, and he didn't think the tapes had been faked. Still... the doubts lingered.

Slowly he said, "I don't have a choice, to tell you the truth."

She smiled coldly. "I'm your last resort, is that it?"

"Look, Miss Pym, I'm prepared to pay you very well. And by the looks of this place, you could use it."

Her back was up at once. "What's that supposed to mean?"

He glanced around the farm, taking in the ramshackle buildings and overgrown weeds. "It means you're broke. Any fool can see the trouble you're in."

"I don't have time to trim rosebushes and paint fences! I've got more important work—"

"Come on, this place is a wreck! The kind of wreck that comes from years of neglect. You expect me to believe this farm is falling apart because you didn't get out your pruning shears yet? And you live in fear of bankers, too."

From between clenched teeth, she said, "My father left some debt, that's all. I'm paying it off."

"With the bank breathing down your neck every step of the way."

"I can handle it."

"Sure," Dash agreed, noting her belligerent stance complete with tight fists and a threatening scowl. She'd be a formidable opponent in any situation, he guessed—as lethal in a knife fight as a marathon weekend in a Pocono honeymoon suite, no doubt. "But why don't you let me ease your burden a little? I'll pay you two thousand dollars."

For a second Molly Pym wasn't sure she'd heard right. Then she almost sat down on the cobblestones. *Two thousand dollars?* Unbelievable! Nobody made that kind of money—at least, nobody Molly had ever met outside the underworld boss she'd once bumped into at a track.

"All right," said the tall man in cashmere when she didn't answer. "I'll make it three thousand."

Molly spun around to keep her expression of amazement to herself. *Three thousand!* Why, that would get the bank off her back for months!

Molly hated being in debt. But the thought of declaring bankruptcy and getting out from under her father's grandiose mistakes had been completely abhorrent to her. The old man's life-insurance policy barely paid the taxes on her property, however, and his pittance of social security went to Molly's mother, living in an inexpensive condo in Florida. Left at home all alone, Molly was starting to lose the battle to hang on to her birthplace. The only asset the old man had left to his daughter was the old Irish magic with horses.

But she couldn't pay bills with magic.

She was too proud to whirl around and accept the three-thousand-dollar offer on the spot. He'd be sure to see her desperation. And the one thing Molly hated more than men asking for her money was a handsome man offering to give her some. It felt wrong. It felt humiliating.

Without turning around, she said, "I only work for myself now."

"Maybe you'll make an exception in this case."

Molly turned slowly and eyed the man who'd come barging into her territory.

He was good-looking in a rugged kind of way. Maybe forty years old, Molly guessed, and very fit. Black hair, strong jaw. She could see the breadth of his shoulders beneath the cashmere sport coat, and noted the way he leaned casually against the fence. Standing that way, he looked like a tiger basking in the sunlight—except not quite so relaxed. There was a certain tension in his body.

Oddly enough, she sensed that his fancy clothes weren't exactly what he would choose to wear on a normal day. Molly could see him in motorcycle leathers or jeans and an old T-shirt. He looked like he'd dressed up for some kind of special occasion he usually shunned. Under the cashmere, he was a tough customer, she suspected.

He used one strong hand to rake back his dark hair, and gazed back at Molly with eyes that were charcoal gray and roiling with barely suppressed tenacity.

He said, "All right, I'll go as high as four thousand—as long as you come right away. I want my colt to start racing as a two-year-old this fall, and we haven't got a moment to lose. You can come to my place tomorrow and begin—"

"I didn't say I'd take the job, pretty boy."

His brow snapped down again.

He was used to having his own way, Molly decided. That's the way rich, handsome men operated. And he was definitely rich as well as handsome. It showed in his good clothes and good manners, though he was obviously having a hard time staying civil.

He was also used to being the boss with women. Molly saw that easily. She'd seen the glimmer of pleasure in his eyes when he'd glanced down at her figure, saw the knowing smile flicker on his mouth when their gazes met. He thought she'd take one look into those devilish, don't-trust-me-in-the-back-seat eyes and cave in. Oh, he expected women to fall at his feet, all right. He expected to find her in his bed very soon indeed.

So Molly took a deep breath and said as plainly as she could, "My answer is no."

"No?" he echoed, his face darkening. Then he growled, "Are you crazy?"

"Nope. I just won't work for you, that's all."

"Why not?"

"Because you're Dash O'Donnelly," she said calmly. "And I'd rather rot in hell than work for the man responsible for my father's death."

Two

——

"Oh, for God's sake!"

Molly didn't trust her self-control and spun around to leave before she punched Dash O'Donnelly in the gut. She marched for the barn, head high.

"Wait!" he called after her. "Surely you don't believe that nonsense."

She kept marching.

"Your father didn't die from anything but natural causes!"

A bad temper was Molly's worst quality—a bad temper where people were concerned, that is. With horses, she could be as patient as pie. But not with human beings. Especially not with men named O'Donnelly.

She swung around and glared. "I know what my father died of, pretty boy. It was betrayal."

"Betrayal?" He gave a laugh of disbelief. "That's rich!"

"He trusted you. He made a deal with you."

"With my father," Dash O'Donnelly corrected.

"You must have been in on the deal, too, and don't deny it!"

"I only know O'Donnelly Farms agreed to share a filly."

"Not just any filly. A great one."

"All horses are great until they step on a track."

Molly refused to hear more. She plunged into the cool barn, but O'Donnelly was hot on her heels.

"That filly wasn't going to amount to much, so we sold her before she became a dead loss."

"You're so sure she wasn't going to amount to anything?"

"That's what my father says, and I have to believe him."

"Well, he's an idiot. An impatient, money-grubbing idiot."

"Time *is* money in this business, Miss Pym."

"Don't patronize *me* about this business, O'Donnelly. You were off climbing mountains or snorkeling in the Bahamas, weren't you? What the hell do you know about what comes with the territory?" Molly racked her brain to remember all the gossip about Dash O'Donnelly—a renegade who'd left the racing world to make his own mark as a professional adventurer. Polo, fast cars, discovering dangerous caverns—he'd done it all in the guise of a writer for glossy magazines. But he'd probably financed his exotic travels using his father's big bucks. "I've heard all about you and your playboy ways!" she snapped.

"You're a rich man's son who spends his life playing games."

A tic showed in O'Donnelly's jaw, and his gaze was hard. "All that's over now."

Molly feigned amazement. "Oh, so you're giving up the jet-set life and coming back to dabble in the family business now? Well, don't expect me to welcome you with open arms, chum. I've lost almost everything because of the O'Donnellys."

"Is it our fault your father didn't keep up his insurance payments?"

That set her off. Molly grabbed a pitchfork out of a hay bale and swung on him, brandishing her weapon. "You and your old man let our filly get into an 'accident' as you call it, knowing full well her death would push my father out of racing for good."

O'Donnelly stood still, unafraid. "That's a damned lie."

"Your father didn't want him around anymore because he was too much competition for you. He was too good!"

"Yes, your old man was very good," Dash said. "But everybody knows he had no head for business. I'm sorry he's dead, but—"

"Oh, save it!"

"Nobody ever said the racing life was fair, Miss Pym."

"Certainly not you or that old horse thief of a father of yours!" Molly felt a rush of tears inside and the pitchfork wavered in her hands. She sucked in a breath for courage. "I bet you'll be pleased to hear that my father's last words were meant for Dillon O'Donnelly. He hoped they'd meet in hell someday!"

Molly threw the pitchfork down with a clatter and cursed her weakness. She leaned back against the nearest stable door and flung up her forearm to dash away any tears that might spill over. It was a struggle, but she held on to her composure. She despised weakness, and the thought of breaking down in front of a man straightened her spine.

In the silence, O'Donnelly picked up the fork and hefted it in one hand with the easy strength of an athlete. After a moment, he said, "I can't change the past, Miss Pym. And I certainly can't bring back your father or even try to make up that loss in your life."

"Oh, shut up!"

He took a step forward and grabbed Molly's arm. She resisted, but he was very strong and pulled until they were toe to toe and she had no choice but to look him in the face. When she reluctantly met his riveting gray gaze, O'Donnelly said, "Maybe I can help you get back on your feet again."

Molly tried to yank out of his grip. "I don't need your damn charity!"

"Maybe not. But I need yours."

"You won't get it!"

"Miss Pym—"

"Nothing's going to change my mind—especially not manhandling!"

He eased up on her arm but didn't let go. "You're sure?"

Molly stuck out her chin. "Absolutely."

"You won't work for me?"

"I'll sweep out cow barns first." She kept her voice steady, but oddly enough, Molly felt herself suddenly tremble in his grasp.

He must have felt that, too, because he looked directly into her eyes again.

"Well, then," he said in a voice that changed timbre. "Maybe I'll have to kidnap you."

The moment stretched, full of his threat. For a split second Molly wasn't sure if he was kidding. And if he wasn't, she might just let him do it. At that thought, a flood of heat rushed up from someplace deep inside her.

"Let me go," Molly said, and she blushed to hear the quiver in her words.

He obeyed a heartbeat later, but neither one of them moved to part. Standing so close, they could hear each other breathe. They could feel a powerful force sizzling in the air between them. Though she'd worked around men all her life and dated a few once in a while, this was the first time she'd ever felt as if she'd been plugged into a light socket. It was crazy. Scary. And hellishly wonderful.

Molly summoned her wits and stepped back, colliding with the closed stable door. She flattened herself against it, wondering what exactly had her brains in an uproar.

O'Donnelly still held the pitchfork in his left hand. Carefully he leaned it against the door beside her. "I wish I could change your mind," he said. "For the sake of Mashed Potato, that is."

"Mashed Potato?"

A small, apologetic smile. "Hell of a moniker, I know. We haven't given him his official name yet. He's a beauty. You should see him. Legs like iron, heart of a lion—oh, he's impossible to describe, really."

Try, Molly wanted to say, glad to have something to think about other than the virility of her father's sworn enemy. Horses were her weakness, and a strong animal with a wild temper never failed to intrigue her. Listening to O'Donnelly as he spoke of his colt, Molly found herself hungering to see this wonder. Just one little peek.

O'Donnelly continued casually. "He can run rings around anything my father's ever seen. He spends his days galloping up and down the pasture, racing the wind. My father's had to cut down on his work and can't waste time working with one colt. Despite my lack of qualifications, I've agreed to come home to help."

"Home for how long?"

Once again, he smiled a little. "I've been a wanderer, I'll admit. But the farm needs me at the moment, so I'm here. I just wish I had the ability to do something with this colt. He'd be magnificent in the right hands."

Dash stole a look at Molly Pym. She was an eyeful, all right. In her twenties, he guessed, and still full of fire. She wanted to throw him out—but he noticed the new light dawning in her eyes. Curiosity. Longing.

Oh, it isn't hard to tempt an Irish girl, he thought with glee. Why hadn't he seen it earlier? Just start rhapsodizing about horses and watch her turn to jelly. No need to kidnap her. Just dangle a tempting horse in front of her nose and lead her anywhere.

With a downcast head and a hint of melancholy, he added, "I wish we had somewhere else to turn, because Mashed Potato is truly a miracle. Pure speed. He absolutely flies. But what a temper! Nasty and brutal—"

"You're just not handling him right," Molly muttered.

"What?"

She smoothed her red hair up from her neck, as if suddenly too hot. She said, "I've never met a horse yet that couldn't be gentled."

Dash shook his head. "We've tried everything we know, and nothing works. If you won't come, I suppose I'll have to..."

"Have to what?" she demanded, back stiffening.

Dash shrugged sadly. "There aren't many alternatives, you know."

She stood straight, hands on hips. "You said yourself he was a miracle. You can't destroy a miracle."

"Well, sooner or later he's going to hurt somebody."

She gave a derisive snort and turned away, striding farther into the barn. A dark horse put his head over the door of the next stall and whickered to her. Automatically Molly put out her hand, and the horse nuzzled it affectionately. Molly glared over her shoulder at Dash. Harshly, she said, "If you're going to get into this business, you'd better develop some compassion for horses."

Dash strolled closer. "Oh, I have compassion, all right. But for the stable hands as much as anything else. Mashed Potato's going to murder one of them." He patted the neck of her horse.

She gave him another look, and Dash decided she was actually beautiful despite all her attempts to remain unfeminine. Though her clothes were rough, those flashing blue eyes and that mouth that trembled at the corners when she was angry—yes, she was quite a woman, all right, full of gutsy confidence and a natural sexiness impossible to fake. The wisps of red hair that caressed the nape of her neck were so tempting that he almost reached out and wound a lock around his finger. Instead, he rubbed her horse.

She said, "Racehorses aren't malevolent."

Dash put on a hopeful expression. "Do you think so?"

"He's probably frightened. Or he's developed a psychological connection between people and something unpleasant."

"I wish I knew what it was." Dash sighed and went on caressing the neck of her horse. He mused, "It's too bad you can't give him a chance."

She was silent.

Cautiously Dash added, "I mean, you could probably take one look at him and know how to fix the problem."

No response.

Dash wasn't much of an actor, but he tried a sigh again—this one full of pent-up sorrow. "I understand your feelings, of course. People—especially family—are more important than horses."

She began to tap the toe of her boot. Gruffly she muttered, "I suppose I could take a couple of hours and run up to your place."

"What?"

She shrugged. "The least I can do is take a look at him."

Got her! Hastily Dash reined in his delight and said solemnly, "Well, that's very generous of you, Miss Molly."

She flashed another glare at him. "It's not generous. It's downright selfish. I want to see this animal

for myself. But I won't speak to your father, understand?''

"I could probably keep him out of your way.''

"Promise,'' she snapped. "Because if I see him, I
might try killing him.''

"It's a deal,'' Dash vowed, hoping to hell he could
keep that promise. Handling an explosive Molly Pym
was only slightly more difficult than handling Dillon
O'Donnelly.

Molly continued. "And I'm not saying I'll do anything, understand? I'll just take a look at the colt.
Don't try tricking me into doing more.''

"I wouldn't dream of it.''

"*And* it's going to cost you five hundred dollars.
Call it a consulting fee.''

"A bargain, I'm sure,'' Dash replied.

No handshake was forthcoming, but another of
those long electrified moments happened then. For an
odd second Dash felt the unmistakable pull of sexual
attraction from Molly Pym. He had knocked around
the world long enough to appreciate the rarity of such
an occurrence. It was pure chemistry—the combina-
tion of just the right elements at just the right time to
cause an exciting reaction. Sometimes an explosion.

Some women bristled with sexual signals. But this
one wore hers deeper—beneath a shield of protection
that masked a certain vulnerability, too.

Watch out, he thought to himself. This one's complicated. *She'll get under your skin before she gets into
your bed, Dash, my man.*

The moment ended when her dog suddenly started
to bark outside.

"Now what?''

Molly pushed the horse's head away, clearly just as relieved as Dash was that the flash of sexual signals had passed. "Somebody's coming."

"Maybe I started a rush on business."

"I doubt it," she retorted. In a few quick strides, she arrived at the open door and looked out into the cobblestone yard. "Look, don't take this the wrong way, O'Donnelly," she said, keeping an eye on the lane, "but how about making yourself scarce?"

"What's the matter?"

"Nothing. It's— Oh, it's probably the guy from the bank."

"So?"

"So I'd rather do business with him alone, if you don't mind."

Dash shrugged. "Okay, it's time I was leaving any-way—"

"Wait!" She grabbed his sleeve, then immediately let go as if she'd been burned. Her cheeks were suddenly pink again. "Listen, there's no time to explain, but couldn't you just disappear? Before he sees you, I mean. I don't want the bank to know you were here."

"Why not?"

She scowled fiercely. "I don't owe you any explanations! Just go wait up at the house, all right? Go through those bushes." She pointed to a tangle of weeds.

"Miss Pym—"

"Go, damn it!"

"I have nothing to hide."

"But *I*— Oh, hell, you don't owe me anything, but couldn't you just get out of sight for five minutes?"

When she turned a desperate face up to him, Dash almost laughed. "As a favor, you mean?"

Her fists tightened, but she said, "As a favor, yes."

He considered asking for the magic word, but something in her expression told Dash she'd rather die than be polite to him. And he wasn't interested in breaking her spirit. He liked the flash of fire that glowed inside Molly Pym. "Okay," he said after the briefest hesitation. "I'll hide at the house."

"Great. Now move it!"

She shoved him, hard. Without knowing exactly why, Dash headed into the bushes and skulked in the direction of the house.

He reached the shelter of a riotous rosebush in the nick of time. In the next instant, a short man in a business suit rounded the curve in the lane, mopping his balding forehead with a white handkerchief. Molly walked down to meet him, her back stiff.

Staying out of sight, Dash found himself on an old flagstone terrace with thick moss growing up between the cracked stones and a tangle of rosebushes closing in on all sides. It had once been a charming spot, he guessed, but nature was slowly taking over. Dash snagged his jacket on a thorny branch before gaining the relative safety of the porch. There he ducked behind a pillar to avoid being seen by the visiting banker.

But the porch wasn't very interesting, and the unlocked screen door was more of a temptation than Dash could resist.

What kind of woman was Molly Pym? In his travels, he had never met anyone quite as tough *and* touchy as she was. Here was an unlocked door, a veritable invitation to learn more about her.

To satisfy his curiosity, Dash eased open the door and let himself into her house.

He found himself in a foyer that had been pleasant in its day. But the wooden floor creaked underfoot, and peels of ceiling paint hung like spiderwebs from the warped crown molding. Dash saw a bare spot on one wall and knew it could only have been the location of a painting long ago. Had the artwork been hocked? he wondered.

And the whole house was damn cold, despite the warm summer sunshine outside. The frugal Miss Molly wasn't wasting a penny on heat or light. The only illumination in the foyer came from the rays of sunlight that slanted through the leaded-glass side windows.

He peeked into the darkened sitting room and saw the curly shapes of ancient Victorian furniture complete with antimacassars. Lace curtains hung in the windows, and bits of colored glass decorated the mantel. It was a very pretty room, but obviously rarely used. A fine layer of dust seemed to coat every surface.

Here was a side of the horse-racing industry Dash had never seen before. His own father trained horses for Arab sheikhs and European royalty. But some trainers—even good trainers like Paddy Pym—barely scraped out a living. The aged house with its dusty furniture and overgrown bushes told a story that was new to Dash.

He strolled through the room and found himself standing before a pair of handsomely carved pocket doors. He slid them open, sure he was going to find an equally dreary dining room on the other side.

But the table and china breakfront had been pushed aside and the room reorganized into a makeshift bedroom.

And what a bedroom!

Dash grinned. "Well, well, Miss Molly."

He sauntered through the doors and looked around. A huge Victorian bed stood square in the middle of the room, covered with a mountain of eyelet lace and a dozen faded chintz pillows. Dash ran his fingers along a frilly canopy that had been fashioned out of some old lace curtains. A soft scent wafted from an antique lady's vanity table where an assortment of delicate crystal bottles flanked a carved oval mirror.

Dash tried to picture the gruff Miss Molly Pym asleep in that ocean of femininity, wearing only subtle perfume and lounging on the flowered pillows. Though she had the body of a bombshell, he'd never expected her to have a romantic side.

"What's this?"

He picked up a wisp of pink lace from the bedpost and found himself staring at a sexy little teddy—the kind of garment he had a hard time imagining on Molly's lean, unyielding body.

To himself, Dash murmured, "Maybe she has a sister."

He heard a thump on the porch and bolted like a burglar caught in the act. He skidded into the sitting room and slid the carved doors closed behind him just in time.

Molly burst into the room, breathless and angry.

With a start, Dash realized he still had her pink teddy clutched in his hand. He whipped it behind his back and endeavored to look innocent. "How'd it go?"

"Great," she said, her voice dripping with sarcasm. She ripped a bandanna from her hip pocket and swabbed her neck of perspiration. "He thinks I own

the fancy car that's parked down by my gate. He tells
me it's worth more than the mortgage on this farm. I
told him he could have it."

"I still have the keys. He couldn't have taken it."

"Well, he *wanted* to."

"Late on a payment?" Dash guessed.

"It's worse than that," she muttered, then stopped
herself from saying more. The idea of an O'Donnelly
hearing about her final warning from the bank was
obviously hard to swallow. "It's none of your business," she said curtly. "Are you finished here,
O'Donnelly?"

"Do we still have a deal?"

"Sure, sure. I'll be at your place this afternoon."

"Maybe I ought to take you with me in my car."

She slanted a wry look up at him. "Afraid I'll back
out?"

"No," Dash said honestly. He prided himself on
being a good judge of character, and he pegged Molly
for a straight citizen. But he didn't feel like leaving.
Not yet. He was just starting to see behind the protec-
tive facade Molly kept in place, and he wanted to learn
more.

Deciding on the spur of the moment, he resorted to
an old ploy. "Have you got something to drink? A
glass of water, maybe?"

Suspicion burned in her eyes, but eventually she
shrugged. "Sure. Kitchen's this way. I don't spend
much time in here."

Dash guessed Molly lived in as few rooms as possible to save on expenses. She led the way out of the old
sitting room, through the drafty foyer and into the
back of the house where the kitchen lay. It was a sun-
nier space than the front of the house, with tall win-

dows and an old white porcelain stove standing in the corner. The walls were painted a fresh yellow. Pots of herbs lined a windowsill, and a lumpy but comfortable-looking sofa had been dragged into a spot near the brick fireplace. It was heaped with magazines, notebooks and unopened mail—bills, mostly, Dash noticed. A tangle of bits and bridles lay on the table with a tin of saddle soap and some cleaning rags. He had guessed right. She lived in the kitchen and used the adjacent dining room as a lady's bedchamber.

Molly plucked a drinking glass off a wooden draining rack and ran water from the tap. While her back remained turned, Dash slipped her teddy into his jacket.

"There," she said, turning to him again. "Cool off."

Wondering if she'd guessed his state of mind, Dash accepted the glass. He avoided a chip in the rim and sipped the water. Cool and sweet. He kept his eyes on her face, though, and decided that Molly Pym wasn't cool or sweet. Hot and spicy, he suspected.

"Better?" she asked, returning his look with one brow raised.

"Getting there." He sipped more water. "Are you going to tell me why I had to hide from your banker?"

She turned away and pretended to reorganize the bridles on the table. "I just didn't want him seeing you around the place. He's already hoping I'll find a fairy godmother to pay my bills, and you might look like the answer to his—well, I don't want to get his hopes up, that's all."

"That's all?" he repeated.

"It's all you need to know."

"I was just curious."

You're not the only one, Molly almost said. She made a business of unbuckling a bit from its bridle and wondered why she hadn't ordered Dash O'Donnelly off her property yet. He might be good-looking, but he was still a damned O'Donnelly, and that should have gotten him tossed off the premises an hour ago. But Molly couldn't bring herself to do it.

Affecting a casual tone, she asked, "Are you going to tell me why you're taking over your father's operation?"

"I'm not taking over," O'Donnelly said at once. "I'm not trained for it."

"Any fool can see that," she retorted.

He laughed shortly. "You sound like my father."

Molly skewered him with a look. "Your father must be really sick if he's letting you into his domain."

"He's getting older," O'Donnelly admitted, strolling to the sink and leaning against it.

"Are you planning to step into his shoes? Take over the operation?"

Dash smiled at her over the rim of his water glass, and for a moment he looked wickedly amused. "For generations, my family has been involved in one of two businesses," he said. "Horses or gambling. My great-grandfather was one of the founders of the Saratoga racing season, you know—a bit of a trick, considering the government had conscripted all horses for use in the Civil War. But he managed to scrape up enough for the Saratoga season. It wasn't from his love of animals, though."

"He was a gambling man," Molly guessed. "And you are, too?"

Dash nodded once. "I'm afraid so."

"But gambling's illegal. Most of it, anyway."

"Not the kind I do."

"Ah, yes," she said, recalling what she'd heard about the younger O'Donnelly over the years. The O'Donnelly clan was always good for racetrack gossip, and Molly had sat in on enough poker games during her life to know a lot of O'Donnelly history. "Mountain climbing and deep-sea fishing. Downhill ski racing and fast cars at Daytona. Those are all forms of gambling, aren't they?"

O'Donnelly smiled lazily. "I like to think so."

"Do you make a living at that kind of thing? Or does dear old dad finance your fun?"

"I get along. Magazines pay me to do things and write about them. But it's not the money that keeps me going."

"The risk," Molly guessed, noting the gleam in his eye.

"The adventure," Dash corrected, meeting her gaze.

She turned away hastily. "And now racing's going to be an adventure for you, is that it?"

"Maybe," he said. "That depends on you, I guess."

Molly leveled a quelling stare at him. "I'm no man's adventure, O'Donnelly."

"You don't like men? Or you're afraid of adventure?"

"I like men fine. But I'm my own boss."

"In all situations?"

"All," she said firmly.

Dash pulled a wisp of pink fabric from inside his jacket. "That's not the impression I got from this."

He might as well have punched her in the stomach.

Molly leapt for him, snatching the garment from his fingers. "Where did you get this? Damn it, you were snooping in my house!"

"Yep," he replied, laughing down at her as she balled up the pink teddy in her hands. "I must say, you're a lot more interesting than the other racetrack types I've met lately. You don't sleep with your horses, I notice."

"You arrogant son of a—"

"Now, now," he soothed. "You were telling me about being the boss. Does that happen in your bedroom, too?"

Humiliated and very angry, she snapped, "Go to hell!"

"I'm probably headed there," he said, damned agreeable and playing the charming rogue. "Tell me about your love life, Miss Molly. I'd like to know who has the pleasure of your company when you're wearing that pretty bit of—"

"Get the hell off my land, O'Donnelly."

"But we were just getting to the good part."

"I should have thrown you out of here a long time ago!"

"Why didn't you?"

Molly wasn't sure how it happened. But suddenly she was standing before him, breathing hard and fighting off the urge to do something very physical. She could read the same urge in O'Donnelly's face, too, plain as day. She couldn't speak, couldn't move.

Softly he taunted, "Why didn't you throw me out?"

"Because—because—"

"You like adventure, too, don't you?"

"I'm too busy trying to stay alive—something you'd never understand, I'm sure."

O'Donnelly set down his glass. "I understand more than you think."

He grabbed Molly by her arms and pulled until her body was flush with his. The heat of him burned through their clothes, and she could feel the tensile strength in his legs and chest. He was very strong—a man capable of climbing mountains. She pressed her hands against him, and suddenly felt the hammer of his heartbeat beneath her palms. Her own pulse was out of control, too.

He bent to kiss her, and Molly reacted instantly, turning rigid and glaring up at him. "Don't."

"I will," he murmured. "I'm a fool for doing it, but I will because you want it as much as I do."

He didn't take the kiss, though. He hovered above her for an agonizing moment—gray eyes alight, hands tight upon her, his body braced. Though she held her breath and fought down the urge, desire twisted sharply inside Molly.

"See?" O'Donnelly said softly. "There's something going on, isn't there? Something sexy and exciting."

"I don't know what you're talking about."

He remained close—teasingly close—his mouth mere centimeters from taking hers. But he didn't kiss Molly. He waited while the passion brewed inside her, watching her eyes. Then Molly let out an unsteady breath, and he moved.

His mouth found hers with surprising gentleness—aching gentleness—wetting the surface of her lips with a flick of his tongue first, then pressing slowly until they were deeply fused. With a deliciously erotic circular motion, he managed to go deeper still and melt all of Molly's reserves.

Although her brain insisted she resist, another part of her cried out to yield. She listened to that softer voice, relishing the kiss until she found herself responding—enjoying the texture, the taste, the heat. She didn't care who he was or why he'd come. He was *here* and that was all that mattered. All the worry and tension that had been mounting for weeks suddenly boiled over.

He felt marvelous against her—tall and strong. Molly surrendered to the pull of sensual pleasure as all her senses reached out to him. Crazily her hands crept up the contour of his chest and found the powerful column of his throat, the curve of his neck, the thick growth of dark hair at the back of his head.

He groaned as she pressed closer still, and her breasts settled against his chest. Her right thigh slid instinctively between his knees. It felt so good, so right, such a relief to let go. Dash skimmed one hand down to the small of her back and used that leverage to arch Molly even more delightfully against him. She loved it and let all resistance go up in smoke.

She wasn't sure how long it lasted. Locked in that embrace, they kissed for a wonderful, timeless moment. But a voice began to scream in the back of her mind and slowly Molly regained her senses. Reluctantly she pushed at his shoulders. Dash obeyed the silent command, though when he pulled back, he was out of breath.

"That's enough," Molly managed to say, unable to meet his eyes. She reached for the table to support herself. Her knees were trembling.

"Not for me."

"I can't do this."

"Because of who I am?"

"For lots of reasons." One of which was fear. In Molly's current state of mind, she wasn't sure she could stop herself if things got out of hand.

"This isn't over, you know."

"Yes, it is."

He laughed—still breathless and touching one knuckle to the corner of his mouth as if to hold the flavor of their kiss there a little longer. "If you believe that, you're not as smart as I think you are, Miss Molly. I'll see you later this afternoon."

"No—"

"You agreed to look at my colt."

"I won't come."

"Yes, you will. I'll see you at three."

He left without another word.

When she heard the front door slam, Molly shakily sank down onto one of the kitchen chairs. She put her head into her hands and tried to catch her breath, thinking a thousand thoughts at once. Kissing a man an hour after she'd met him. Kissing an *O'Donnelly*, for crying out loud! A handsome, sexy O'Donnelly who could read her mind! And of all things, she'd agreed to meet him again.

She'd call it off. The hell with him. Let him keep his five hundred dollars.

Five hundred dollars. That was money that would go a long way right now.

Molly closed her eyes and moaned, dropping her head down on the tabletop. "I need the money, and I need it bad."

She'd have to go to O'Donnelly Farms to get it. And she could only hope to heaven he'd keep his distance once she got there. Molly had a feeling she wasn't strong enough to resist him on her own.

Three

Dash sat through an interminable luncheon of the Racing Committee without hearing a word of the discussion.

He sat there picturing Molly Pym in her big Victorian bed.

He even groaned over his chicken croquettes, drawing a puzzled look from the rest of the table before banishing the images that robbed him of his concentration.

He wanted to see her again. Soon. It was strange, but the need to feast his eyes on Molly Pym—to hear her voice again and feel her body against his—couldn't be suppressed. Oh, she was dangerous, all right. In less than an hour, she'd reached inside Dash and grabbed a part of him that had been declared dead a long time ago. It was more than sex—though Dash told himself that sex was foremost in his mind.

He began to wish he *had* kidnapped her.

In his car again and racing homeward, he muttered to himself, "If only I can keep her away from Pop."

Dillon O'Donnelly was going to have a fit when he laid his eyes on Paddy Pym's daughter.

Contemplating exactly how he was going to avoid such a confrontation, Dash drove through picturesque Saratoga. Although the racing season wasn't due to get under way for another month, the town was bedecked with flower boxes and bunting. New paint sparkled on the intricate Victorian trim of gracious homes. Tourists spilled out of trendy bistros.

In another few weeks the streets would be crowded with celebrities hoping to be recognized, heiresses in their pearls and broad-brimmed hats, New Yorkers on holiday. Old money. The horsey set. Dash had been away just long enough to enjoy the color of his hometown again.

Fifteen miles out of town lay O'Donnelly Farms, a venerable racing stable that would have looked right in Kentucky or the English countryside. Dash drove through the security gate, waving at the guard, then roared up the lane to the center of the complex.

He took refuge in his office—a large suite of rooms located across a paved private road from the North Barn where the O'Donnelly stallions were stabled.

After checking through the mail with his father's faithful and efficient secretary, Dash went into his office, closed the door and lit a cigar. With his loafers propped on the fine mahogany surface of his desk, he smoked and considered his position.

Life certainly had a way of changing direction in ways a man didn't expect. A year ago he'd been preparing to race a car in France—a job he'd accepted as a favor to a friend who manufactured the fine sports cars. But a chance phone call home to his father—a call in which the old man sounded confused—had changed Dash's mind. He had responsibilities in life and a heritage to hang on to. A crash at the beginning of the race seemed to make the point even more strongly. So now he was back home at O'Donnelly Farms, trying to keep the peace and get the financial affairs back in some kind of order. Dash's father *had* been confused. Dash was startled to see what bad shape things were in. And now it was his job to wave a magic wand and fix all the problems his father's advancing years had caused. It wasn't an easy job, but he tackled it with vigor.

As he mused, Dash allowed his idle gaze to wander over the framed pictures on the opposite wall—pictures of O'Donnelly horses draped in their winning blankets of flowers; O'Donnelly studs staring nobly into the distance while smiling grooms held their reins; and O'Donnelly mares standing with frisky young foals at their sides. By God, they were superb.

Dash's father had ordered the pictures hung in the new office the day he'd moved in, obviously hoping that Dash would develop some family pride by staring at the collection of photos.

Dash *did* feel pride. Although he'd cleared out as soon as he was old enough to get out from under his father's domination, he loved the farm and fiercely hoped he could save it.

But today he found himself feeling something else.

And it had to do with Molly Pym.

She stuck in his mind like a burr. Why now, when Dash knew it should be consumed by the financial problems of the farm? It seemed unreasonable, but he couldn't stop thinking about her. She was a prickly thing, he thought. Hot-tempered. And hot-blooded, too. The glimpse into her bedroom had suggested that and thrust Dash's imagination into overdrive.

He pushed her to the back of his mind, but she kept returning. How might she look with her hands scrubbed, her hair combed and that tight look of control washed off her face by some gentle lovemaking? How did her pretty pink nightie skim her curves? He could almost feel her body against his again, and he imagined peeling those silky straps off her shoulders to reveal her small but very firm breasts.

"Dad!"

The boy who burst into the office had no idea what kind of scenario he was interrupting. Dash sat up hastily.

His eight-year-old son looked like a cross between a street urchin and a rap singer who'd gotten dressed in a dark closet. The boy's loose shorts flapped around his skinny legs, and his neon T-shirt was big enough to clothe a professional linebacker. Obviously he'd been dressed by his older brother that morning, and the effect was one of a mismatched pickpocket. The laces on his enormous sneakers trailed behind as he flung himself breathlessly through the door. His face was framed by a pair of black plastic spectacles that gave the boy an unsettling googly-eyed look.

"Dad, I'm warning you! You've got just enough time to slip out of here, but you gotta move fast!"

Coming back to O'Donnelly Farms had thrust Dash into another role that had eluded him for a long time—that of father to his three children. During a marriage that had essentially been one of convenience between himself and Billie, Dash had never been a custodial parent. Billie hadn't seemed to expect it during their twelve-year on-again-off-again marriage, and after the divorce she'd appeared to want him to keep his distance in order to promote peace in her own family. Billie's upper-crust New York clan was relieved to have Dash out of their daughter's just-so life and had taken over the job of raising the children to live in their world.

But Billie had gone off like a whirlwind to Europe for the summer in another move that horrified her proper parents. And, in an uncharacteristic moment of autonomy, she'd disobeyed her family's wishes and left the children in Dash's charge, claiming it would be good for all of them.

Knowing Billie, she had a more complicated agenda on her mind. She hadn't always been under her family's collective thumb. After all, she *had* married Dash and taken him home like some kind of big-game trophy. Trouble was, Dash hadn't fit in at the family's Park Avenue apartment or the summer house on the ocean. All Billie's girlfriends had swarmed around him, causing a few too many embarrassing moments, and Dash had had a hard time making small talk about the stock market, modern painters and charity balls. He'd figured out very early that an unconventional husband was part of a plan Billie had hatched to get attention. Billie was always hatching plans. She was clever, just not always strong enough to see things through.

But Dash didn't take time to wonder about Billie's current plan just then. He contrived to look like a disapproving father and said to his son, "Montgomery, you're behaving like a wild man again."

"Save the lectures, Dad." Montgomery was exasperatingly verbal and quick-witted for an eight-year-old. It came from hanging around his teenage brother and a sly older sister who was on the verge of a hormonal cataclysm. Montgomery planted his grubby hands on the desk and leaned over it, panting dramatically. "I'm telling you, it's time to get your rear in gear. The old man's coming!"

In a voice he hoped Billie's family would approve of, Dash said sternly, "I won't have you calling your grandfather names, young man."

Montgomery's eyes popped wide with horror. "Well, I'm not sticking around here for another one of his lectures. He's worse than my other grampa! He *yells!* Catch you later—and don't say I didn't warn you!"

Before Dash could protest, Montgomery took his leave by pushing open the window and leaping for freedom. He landed in the rhododendron bush outside and yelped. But he must have been okay, because a second later Dash heard him scrambling to escape.

Dash considered following.

But he hesitated just ten seconds too long.

Dillon O'Donnelly threw open the office door and entered the room in a single stride. He was a proud, hale Irishman laying claim to his turf, a Roman emperor stepping onto the field of battle, a man of action ready to act. Broad-shouldered, red-faced and full of fire.

"Young man," he roared, "where is that conniving son of yours? I saw him come in here a minute ago, so don't deny it!"

Dash did not move from his seemingly relaxed position, blew a cloud of smoke and regarded his father calmly. "Which conniving son do you mean, Pop? I have two."

"And neither one of them is going to live up to the O'Donnelly name unless you start using a firm hand! That ex-wife of yours can't control them, so it's up to you!" Dillon slammed the office door and threw himself into a spate of angry pacing, his boots trailing stable straw all over the handsome carpeting.

Dash couldn't help but admire the old coot. For a man of nearly eighty years, Dillon was amazingly virile. He spent every day of his life working eighteen hours in the stables, slaving much harder than any employee. His only concession to physical weakness was a slight limp he retained after a kick from a testy Triple Crown winner.

He had other weaknesses, of course. His impressive physique and loud bluster covered a great many problems that were worsening as Dillon aged. He'd never had a head for figures and his impatience with paperwork increased as he got older. Dillon might have run O'Donnelly Farms into the ground within the next five years—if Dash hadn't come home to supervise things. Even now, Dash had doubts that the farm could be salvaged. Along with trainers like Paddy Pym, Dillon had long believed in intangibles like heart and history. But history didn't pay bills, and Dash's first look into his family's finances had escalated into big bucks.

Dillon didn't give a damn about details. He groused, "I don't understand how you could let that woman get away with such sloppy handling of those children! They're nuisances—all three of them!"

"Billie did a good job, if you ask me," Dash said easily. "They're all smart and seem happy enough. What more do you want?"

"Good manners, for one thing!"

"Why? Nobody else around here has them—yourself included. What's really bugging you, Pop? Something going on?"

"Oh, the usual!" Dillon waved off the inquiry impatiently. "That damned accountant turned up again while you were out. How am I supposed to remember every bookkeeping entry? He was pestering me about taxes I paid three years ago! What kind of accountant wastes his time on the past?"

Accountants who were trying to clean up messes made by old men who should have left their bookkeeping to the experts, Dash thought. But he didn't say so.

"I'll talk to him," he said to his father. "There's probably some mix-up, that's all."

Dillon's craggy face settled deeper into a scowl. "No human being should be expected to remember every check he ever wrote!"

"Right. Want a cigar, Pop?"

The technique worked. Dillon forgot about his accountant and allowed Dash to choose a cigar for him from the humidor on the desk. Although father and son had shared little during the early years, they could both appreciate a fine cigar. With a grudging grin, Dillon accepted one and slid into one of the leather chairs placed in front of the desk. It took him several minutes to get the cigar lit properly, but then he blew smoke contentedly.

"Listen, Pop," Dash began with caution, "I've been thinking about Mashed Potato again."

"He's sure a beauty, isn't he?"

Dash nodded. "Yep."

"I've never seen a colt quite like him."

Patiently Dash listened to his father as Dillon began to list the colt's best qualities. Dillon was full of respect for Mashed Potato's abilities, but he also believed that the horse couldn't be tamed, couldn't be raced and couldn't even be tied to a fence without pulling the posts out of the ground and running all over Saratoga, making a spectacle of himself and fools of his owners. He was a wild and destructive horse, according to Dillon—a devil with a mane and a tail.

Dash, on the other hand, knew the colt was the only thing that was going to save O'Donnelly Farms from bankruptcy.

"We ought to sell him to the knacker," Dillon declared.

Dash studied his own cigar for a while and said, "I'm not giving up on him, Pop. Not yet."

Dillon gave him a crude grin. "You never did know when to cut your losses, boyo. That's what broke your leg in Switzerland. What the hell were you doing there, anyway? I forget."

"Following the downhill champion with a video camera strapped to my skis. I was keeping up, too, until I hit that—well, it doesn't matter now. Listen, Pop, Mashed Potato's a valuable asset to the farm."

Dillon propped his boots up on the desk. "Never a quitter, are you? Well, that's not such a bad thing. You've grown up pretty well, haven't you?"

I had to get away from you to do it, Dash nearly said.

Dillon grinned. "What desperate measures are you taking now? Hiring another crazy animal head shrinker like that goofball from California?"

Dash withheld a sigh. He'd tried to tame Mashed Potato with a variety of remedies—most of them wasting valuable O'Donnelly cash. "No, no head shrinker this time. Nor am I bringing in an expensive quack from England to mix potions out of herbs and roots."

Dillon had the grace to look embarrassed by the fiasco he'd engineered. "All right, what *have* you done?"

Dash took the cigar from his mouth, slid his feet off the desk and leaned forward on his elbows. "You have to promise to stay calm, Pop."

"Stay calm? What for?"

"We agreed the horse is mine now, right? He's not part of your string anymore, he's my colt. You agreed."

Dillon's face began to darken. "Just what have you done, boyo?"

"I'm going to hire someone. A woman. An expert in problem colts. She's the best."

"And?"

"And what?"

"Let the other shoe drop, boyo. What's wrong with her?"

"She's Paddy Pym's daughter."

As if electrified, Dillon leapt from his chair. He stood over the desk, breathing hard and choking with inarticulate fury. He pointed a shaking finger at Dash. "You—you—"

"She's coming this afternoon, and I'd appreciate it if you'd stay clear—"

"You're no son of mine!" Dillon exploded.

"Pop—"

"I won't have a Pym set foot on my property!"

"*Our* property," Dash corrected, for his father had legally given Dash half the assets and most of the control of O'Donnelly Farms when he'd returned.

But Dillon hadn't given up laying down the law. "I'll shoot her on sight!"

Dash tried not to grin as he remembered the sign on Molly Pym's gate. "Maybe you'll get along with her better than I thought. Listen, Pop, I think it's time to put a foolish feud behind us, all right? Paddy's gone now, and he never meant any harm—"

"No harm!"

"He's dead, for crying out loud. You ought to forgive—"

"Don't tell me how to run my life," Dillon snapped. "You may have come back here to clean up a few of my mistakes, boyo, but you'll never understand the likes of Paddy Pym."

"All right," Dash shot back, "but Mashed Potato is under *my* jurisdiction now, and I'm going to hire Molly Pym to train him."

"You'll live to regret it, boyo!"

Dillon always got in the last word. He stormed out of the office and banged the door behind him.

Dash put the cigar back in his mouth and looked up at the ceiling. "Well, that went better than I thought it would," he said to himself.

Molly Pym appeared about an hour later.

In a rattletrap pickup truck that made more noise than a Sherman tank, she pulled through the gates of O'Donnelly Farms and roared up the lane like an invading army. The brakes shrieked horribly as she stopped in front of Dash's office. By the time he heard the spluttering engine cough and die, Dash was already on the porch to greet her.

Her ancient vehicle looked like an eyesore in the midst of the surrounding O'Donnelly splendor, but Molly got out of the truck looking thunderously proud. Just seeing her slam the truck door made Dash smile. A smattering of rust fell off the truck when the door slammed, but she pretended not to notice. Her three-legged dog happily sat panting on the front seat—another eyesore.

Several human heads and a few equine ones poked out of the nearest stable to see what all the commotion was about.

"You want me to park this someplace special?" Molly demanded when she saw Dash come out to greet her.

"I'll have somebody take care of it," he said smoothly, going down the steps with his hand extended. "Welcome to O'Donnelly Farms, Miss Molly."

She took his handshake in a firm grip, but he thought he detected a tremble when the contact lasted just a fraction of a second too long. Dash noticed she had washed her face, but hadn't changed her clothes. She felt no need to get all gussied up for a trip to a horse barn, and he liked her no-nonsense appearance—especially now that he knew she had a romantic side. Her bright hair had been windswept during the truck ride, and her golden skin shone in the afternoon sunlight. She looked fresh and untamed—a woman worth pursuing.

But Dash saw a flicker of unease in the back of her blue eyes. It surprised him, then warmed his heart.

Her scowls and harsh words were nothing but smoke screen. Inside, Dash was willing to bet she was as soft as marshmallow fluff.

"Got a problem, O'Donnelly?"

He realized he had been admiring her figure again and let go of her hand. "Why do you ask?"

Tartly, she said, "You're looking at me like you haven't had a decent meal in weeks. Didn't you get any food at that highbrow luncheon today?"

"Maybe I'm not hungry for food."

She let that one pass and glanced around the immaculate landscape and the perfectly maintained stables of O'Donnelly Farms. Dash tried to imagine what she was seeing in comparison to her own farm, and guessed that the abundance of flowers, the freshly whitewashed fences and the sparkle of polished brass must have startled her eye. Everything must have looked expensive to her. A few steps away, one of the O'Donnelly employees was unloading a mare who was at the farm to visit one of their stallions. Only Dash knew how desperately the farm needed the cover fee that came with the mare.

A deep-chested neigh resounded from the stallion barn, and the mare pricked her ears. Dash smiled, for sexual attraction between horses meant money in the bank.

Molly tilted her head to listen to the stallion for a moment, then kicked a nearby flowerpot with the scuffed toe of her riding boot. "This is a pretty fancy place you've got, O'Donnelly. When does your butler serve tea?"

"Later," Dash said. "On the veranda, as a matter of fact. Today we have a visitor from some Middle East country, a sheikh who wants to buy a horse. You can meet him, if you want. But the butler's a woman who's been in the family for years."

She looked like she wasn't sure whether to believe him or not. To be on the safe side, she changed the subject. "When do I see the colt?"

Molly knew she'd better keep her mind focused on why she'd come. But just one look at Dash O'Donnelly had her insides in an uproar again. Did he have to be so damned attractive? Standing there in the sunshine, he could have been a movie star—one of those larger-than-life heroes who played cops or spies or supermen. When he'd grasped her hand, she had struggled to keep a blush at bay. What an idiotic thing to do—blush over a man!

A warm sensation lingered in her breasts and belly, and when she met his gaze, the heat began to spread in tingles through her limbs to the tips of her fingers and toes. It was uncontrollable. And maddening.

A light of amusement entered Dash's eyes. He knew exactly what she was feeling.

Then he seemed to collect himself. "Come on, I'll show you the colt right away, if you like."

"That's the only reason I came."

He laughed, damn him, but led the way across a perfectly level paved lane to a five-bay garage full of beautifully maintained vehicles. In the cool dimness, Molly spotted a low slung sports car, a wide-base pickup truck, a station wagon and a Jeep. Against the rear wall stood a well-used motorcycle.

Molly gestured to it. "Yours?"

He nodded and opened the passenger door of the Jeep for her. "But this is a better way to get where we're going today. Hop in."

Molly climbed into the Jeep without accepting Dash's outstretched hand for assistance. When she was in the seat and he had closed the door, she stuck her thumb and forefinger in her mouth and let loose an earsplitting whistle.

From across the lane, Seabiscuit gave a happy bark and jumped out of the pickup. He bounded across the pavement and in a single leap cleared the side of the Jeep and landed with his dirty paws in the back seat of Dash's perfectly clean vehicle.

Dash looked momentarily dismayed. "He's coming with us?"

"Biscuit goes everywhere with me. You got an objection?"

"Of course not," he said, but looked at the dog with obvious misgivings. "Unless he's hoping to eat some more of my clothes."

"I think you're safe. I fed him before we came over here."

"Let's hope he's not in the mood for dessert." Dash rounded the Jeep and got in behind the wheel. The keys were already in the ignition. Molly guessed he didn't have to worry about anybody stealing his automobiles. She had passed through a security checkpoint and a guarded gate before being allowed to enter the hallowed grounds of O'Donnelly Farms.

Dash started the vehicle with a roar and backed out of the garage smoothly, then threw the Jeep into gear and pulled away from the buildings. Taking the uppermost of three lanes that diverged from the main office, he drove up a small hill. A white split-rail fence ran along either side of the lane, which was shaded by graceful maple trees.

Everywhere Molly looked she saw signs of great wealth. To her, it was obvious the O'Donnelly family had been swimming in cold hard cash for generations. The stable and surrounding countryside looked more like a blue-chip industrial park than a horse farm. Everything was spick-and-span, freshly painted and spit polished to look brand-new.

And the horses! Grazing the pastures that lay all around them, Molly saw exquisite horses. Their sleek coats and brass-plated halters gave them the look of champions, all right. A herd of splendid yearlings galloped around the top of a knoll, playing at winning great races.

A half-a-dozen mares with foals were standing by the fence farther down the lane, and they put their heads over the rails to gaze placidly at the passing Jeep. Molly tried not to think that just one of those fine brood mares might save her own farm from bankruptcy.

It was probably at that moment that Molly decided the O'Donnellys could pay her almost any amount and she'd take it. Just a fraction of their wealth could get Pym Stables back in business.

"What do you think?" Dash asked, breaking across her thoughts.

Molly marshaled her thoughts. "Your mares look fat. You fed them too well last winter."

"They'll trim down now," he assured her.

"What's that?" She pointed at a great bronze statue of a horse that graced the hilltop overlooking the rest of the farm.

"That's Scalloped's grave. My father had the bronze commissioned years ago at the height of Scalloped's career." Dash's voice sounded perfectly modulated, which caused Molly to glance at him. Was it her imagination or had he really cared for Scalloped? He said, "We never intended for it to mark his grave, but—well, it seemed like a good spot for him."

"It is," Molly said, squinting toward the statue, which had been placed with honor on the grounds. "But what's that beside it?"

"What?"

Dash craned to look, then nearly ran the Jeep off the road. He cursed. "That little bastard! I ought to—"

He cut himself off, righted the vehicle and floored the accelerator. But instead of driving overland to the statue, where a boy seemed to be splattering the bronze with paint, Dash kept going along the lane. His knuckles were white on the steering wheel as he drove away from the scene of the crime.

"Who was that?" Molly asked. "It was a kid with a can of spray paint, wasn't it? Defacing your statue!"

"It," said Dash from between clenched teeth, "was my son."

"Your *what?*" Molly stared at him. She had never considered such a possibility. "You're *married?*"

"Divorced," Dash said. "But this summer, I have custody of my three children."

Of course he was old enough to have children. It would have been a little odd if he hadn't. Still, it was a jolt. A little dazed, Molly said, "I never thought—I mean, you don't seem like the fatherly type."

"That's what my kids think, too."

"Not going very well, huh?"

"It's going worse than I ever imagined," Dash growled.

"What's wrong?"

"They have been raised by their mother, who has a hard time with discipline, you see, and they—well, they're hellions."

"Like their father?"

Dash didn't get angry. "I admit, I've been an absent father. But my wife and her family preferred me to show up only for the important occasions."

"Like their conceptions?"

He threw her a wry look. "More than that. I wasn't completely out of their lives, but everyone seemed happier when I was."

"Your wife, too?"

"I think you could say she was relieved."

"She remarried?"

"No, she's a newspaper columnist—society page. That takes up most of her time along with considerable philanthropic work. She's incredibly busy, but I respect what she's managed to do with our children in the face of incredible pressure from her family. And she's a beautiful woman, too."

"Sounds like you married her for more than her beauty."

He laughed. "Well, it's certainly what drew us together in the first place."

"I think she fit your life-style."

He nodded, amused. "That's certainly true. We married young, in rebellion, then we went our separate ways. I was all over the world, while she lived in New York and worked for her family's newspaper. She was a base of operations for me, and although we started our family by accident, it seemed to suit her very nicely."

"And you?"

"What about me?"

"You said you weren't completely out of your children's lives. What are you contributing to their upbringing? Money?"

"Billie comes from a privileged background," Dash said, "so my financial contribution has been a matter of principle only."

"Hmm."

"What does that mean?"

"I was just thinking, that's all."

"You're thinking I've been a terrible father. Well, I admit it. I've dropped into their lives now and then, and that's it. But I can't make up for years of neglect in one summer."

"So you let them get away with spray painting bronze statutes?"

"I'll discuss St. John's actions with him later."

Sinjin. It was the name of a rich kid, Molly thought. A rich, spoiled, headstrong kid whose father was rich, spoiled and headstrong, too. No wonder Dash was having trouble maintaining any kind of control. It must be like trying to control your own unruly passions. And Dash O'Donnelly seemed definitely to have that in spades.

He broke across her brooding by saying blandly, "I didn't hire you to examine my family life, you know."

"You didn't hire me at all," Molly retorted. "Except to take one look at this wonder colt of yours. Where is he? The next county?"

"We keep him in a high pasture where he can't get into any trouble. It's just over this ridge."

The Jeep roared over the last hillock rather the way a roller coaster reaches the crest of its run and balances at the peak for a breathtaking moment. From that highest point, the whole farm was suddenly a

panorama of running fences, emerald green fields and
the black rooftops of stables. On the opposite hillside, however, stood the O'Donnellys' baronial es-
tate, a grand white house with columned porticoes that
overlooked a sparkle of man-made lake. A curved
drive swept up to the front door, and Molly could
picture elegant carriages discharging fancily dressed
guests headed for a hunt ball. She caught a glimpse of
a blue swimming pool and noted a vast flower gar-
den, too.

"Over there," said Dash, as the vehicle plunged
downhill again, "is Mashed Potato."

The wicked son of Scalloped had been given a
meadow fit for a prince among horses. His pasture
was a long, gentle slope of green that could be seen
from the house. A row of thick trees shaded the field,
which was scattered with a carpet of flowers.

Dash drew up the Jeep alongside the tall fence, and
Molly got out as soon as he'd killed the engine.

It only took a moment before he appeared.

The colt made his presence known by first trumpet-
ing a challenging call that echoed among the hillsides.
Then he burst out of the trees like a locomotive, legs
churning in a ground-eating gallop that sounded like
thunder in the still afternoon. He was very dark, with
a red cast to his coat and black points, long-legged,
deep-chested and astonishingly skinny for his height.
His tail, long and black, streamed out behind him like
an airborne rudder as he ran.

"Watch out," said Dash, as the colt cut a corner
and headed directly for them with the speed of a jet on
takeoff. "He's been known to crash fences."

Unafraid, Molly stood transfixed as the animal bore
down on them at a dead run. She marveled at the

length of his stride, the liquid flash of muscle under his sweaty coat. He galloped with all the determination of a guided missile.

Then he jammed on the brakes and skidded to a mud-throwing stop just a dozen yards from where they stood.

Cautiously Molly stepped forward and leaned on the fence to watch.

The colt froze, too, returning Molly's regard with his large, wild eyes fixed on her, his ears pricked forward alertly. His nostrils flared. His head was beautifully carved, his neck curved exquisitely, his shoulders arched with power. But when he stared at Molly, his skin shivered with nerves. His sides heaved, but not with exhaustion.

"He's frantic," Molly said softly, not taking her eyes from the rangy colt.

"Frantic? No, he's just angry all the time."

"It's not anger that makes a young horse look like this. It's something else."

"We're feeding him properly. A little grain, vitamins—"

"It's not that," Molly said impatiently. "First of all, you've got to move him."

"Move him?" Dash objected beside her. "This is the best pasture on the farm! He's got everything he could possibly need—"

"It's not right for him," Molly interrupted. "The wind's wrong."

"The *wind?* Come now, Miss Molly, I'm prepared for a few unusual ideas from you, but—"

"I'm telling you, he's going to die in a month— maybe two—if you leave him like this. He's got no flesh on those bones, just muscle and raw nerves." Her voice rose tensely. "He's upset, and it's going to eat him up. He hates it here. He's completely unanchored."

"Un—?"

"A horse needs a *place,* just like a human being. He's unhappy and scared—but he makes it look like he's angry. All this running around he's doing—it's a search."

Dash watched her as she stared back at the untamed colt. It was impossible, he knew, but the two of them seemed to communicate. A nearly visible crackle of telepathy stretched between the woman and the animal. Two wild and beautiful creatures. The colt reacted by jerking his head higher to get a better view of Molly. And, turning to her, Dash saw something equally fierce reflected in Molly's face, too.

Bewildered, Dash asked, "How can you tell all this?"

"I just can," she whispered.

Puzzled but intrigued, Dash found himself believing her. Maybe it was magic. Maybe it was real. He had nothing left to lose anymore. Dash had to trust Molly Pym and her odd way with horses.

"All right," he said, half-afraid to ask for a definite answer, "will you work with him?"

Molly straightened up and looked at Dash squarely. "Yes, I'll work with him," she said. "But not with you."

"We come as a set, I'm afraid."

"It's a set we'll have to break."

Dash shook his head. "No deal."

Molly's face filled with a desperate eagerness. "But I can *help* him! I can make him feel better, settle him down. I'll take him to my place and—"

"The insurance company says the colt can't leave this farm. You'll just have to stay here with him."

"But—"

"It's not negotiable. You've got us both, Miss Molly, or neither one."

Four

———

He couldn't believe she was so stubborn.

"I can't do it," she said, turning away. "I can't be around you."

Dash stared after her. "Why not? We hit it off, didn't we?"

She stopped in the middle of the road, stiff as she kept her back to him and shoving her hands into the front pockets of her jeans. "Maybe that's the point. I can't concentrate on him if I have to worry about you at the same time."

"What's to worry about?"

"You *know*," Molly cried, spinning around. "It—it's not a working situation at all. It's—"

Firmly, Dash cut across her objections. "Look, you're not a lawyer who's got to be concerned about a conflict of interest. I want you to train a horse. And I like what's happening on the side between you and

me. The two situations have nothing to do with each
other.''

"But—"

"You're a sexy young woman, and I'm attracted to
you."

She winced. "Don't say that."

Dash threw up his hands. "Why not? It's true!"

"It would never work," she snapped.

"Why not? I'm not much older than you. Is that
it?"

"No, no. You're just not my type."

He laughed at that. "What *is* your type? Someone
with four legs and a tail?"

"I'm not just a horse-crazy girl with a father fixa-
tion," she retorted, getting steamed. "I'm a woman,
and I haven't exactly been a nun all my life. But
you—! You want a plaything, O'Donnelly."

"For God's sake—"

"You take women lightly."

"Lightly? Where did you get that idea? From two
minutes of discussion about my life? Hell, it was *her*
idea to split up."

"You're the kind of man who considers sex a form
of exercise."

He had to laugh. "A very exciting form of exercise, you'll admit!"

She didn't smile back. "It's *not* exercise for me. It's
a lot more. And you're incapable of taking the next
step."

"What step is that?"

"Admitting there's something more to making love
than sweat and great orgasms."

At her direct approach, Dash leaned back against
the fence and studied her—a good-looking young

woman with a great body, fiery spirit and a plainspo-
ken attitude about life. She also had an unexpected
streak of romance in her, and it was that part Dash
wanted to avoid at all costs. "I won't pretend I don't
want to make love with you, Miss Molly, if that's what
you call it," he said. "I do. And you're going to meet
me halfway."

She shook her head, red hair glinting in the sun.
"You've got me wrong."

"I don't think so." Dash moved off the fence and
began to stalk her. "You've been thinking about sex
since we met, haven't you?"

She folded her arms across her chest as if to stand
her ground. "I don't want to talk about this."

"Coward," he said softly, getting closer.

Her eyes blazed, but she retreated a step, moving
toward the Jeep. "I'm *not* a coward."

"Prove it."

She blew an impatient sigh. "That's a juvenile
game, and I can't believe you'd stoop to playing it."

"Maybe it's a very grown-up game. It's a very old
one, at least." Dash was gratified to see her take another wary step backward.

"I don't like your game."

He followed her around the parked Jeep, for some
reason suddenly determined to show her the differ-
ence between making love and just plain great sex
without entanglements. Great sex had its good points.
"Men and women have been playing my game since
the beginning of time."

"That makes it right?"

"It makes it exciting."

"Daring each other to take off our clothes isn't my
idea of exciting."

"You'll have to take off more than your clothes, I'm afraid. Your inhibitions have to come off first."

"And your emotional arrogance had better take a hike, too." She backed around the hood of the Jeep, keeping the vehicle between them for safety.

He had to laugh. "Emotional arrogance? What's that?"

"You're playing holier-than-thou. Only, this version is called I'm-not-repressed-and-you-are. Well, any fool can strip naked and screw their brains out, O'Donnelly." She stopped and said tauntingly, "It takes more courage to admit there's something else besides sex hidden behind that cocky grin of yours."

Dash kept his grin in place. "What do you think I'm hiding?"

She rocked on the heels of her boots. "A lot of things. Your true feelings about your children, for starters."

Dash felt a quick tide of anger inside. "Now wait a minute—"

She laughed again. "Coward!"

She was close enough to grab, and Dash did it. "My family life is off-limits," he said harshly, clamping down on her wrist and feeling pleased to sense a surge in her pulse rate.

"Oh, you're setting limits, are you? Is that fair?" she asked archly. "You expect me to give up everything—my principles where my father is concerned, my own farm—everything, so that I can work for you during the day and play your imaginative lover at night?"

"You won't have to give up anything. I'll send someone to manage your farm while you're here."

"What about my father?"

"He's dead, Molly. You can't bring him back."

Her gaze was hot with outrage. "You expect me to simply accept that and jump into your bed?"

"We don't have to use a bed," Dash said, drawing Molly closer. "I could take you into those trees or do it on the grass."

"I don't think so," she said.

"No?" He enjoyed the slender strength of her body against his and slid one hand down her back to cup the delicious curve of her bottom. Hitching her closer yet, he forced her to ride the line of his own frame so that she couldn't mistake the readiness he felt for her. "You don't think I'd do it?"

She shook her head, then touched his face with the backs of her fingertips. It was a light caress, both sexy and soothing. "No, I'm sure of it. You like to think you're a tough guy, Dash O'Donnelly, but you're like that colt over there. You're wild and demanding. But you're hiding something, too. A lot of things."

He longed to kiss her, to press her mouth open and scorch her sassy tongue with his own. But he heard himself murmuring, "Say my name again."

"Dash," she whispered. "Dash."

"Will you kiss me?"

She did it, lifting her lips to his and warming Dash's mouth until he heard himself moan. She wound her arms around his neck and pressed close, learning every contour of his body with her own. Dash moaned again and crushed her to him, suddenly thinking seriously about carrying her off into the woods to be alone with her. He wanted to tear off her clothes and feast his eyes on those tawny limbs, feel them wrap around him. He wanted to get naked with her, touch her, feel her hands on him, too, and finally find the deepest part of her body with long, pulsing thrusts. As if carrying out his plan, both of his hands were suddenly tugging on her shirt and jeans.

She laughed softly against his mouth and writhed in his arms, inflaming Dash with the subtle, rhythmic motion of lovemaking she made as she pressed against him.

The kiss turned hot and hungry as the gates of restraint burst open and they feverishly began to explore each other. Dash tasted a sweet darkness in her mouth, felt the liquid fire of her hair, caressed the lean length of her body. God, she felt good! The things inside her drew him like a magnet—her innate warmth, the brilliance of her spirit. He wanted more.

He maneuvered to get one hand between their two straining chests and found the wonderful roundness of her breast. His thumb urged the nipple to an eager erectness, and she made a soft sound—half gasp, half laugh. When she looked up at him, her eyes were full of desire.

"You're weakening," he said.

"So are you," she replied.

He let her go, surprised. "What do you mean?"

She leaned against the Jeep to get a grip once more. "You talk a good game, O'Donnelly. But you're not as cold-blooded as you like to believe."

"Do you want me to say a lot of empty words?"

She shook her head. "Of course not. I hate anything empty."

"Then why can't we be a couple of mature adults who enjoy each other?"

"Because I can't just go through the motions," she said softly. "And if you can—well, you're more empty than I thought."

"I just want—"

"I know what you want. But I won't let you define me by my sexual performance. I'm *me.*"

"So I've noticed," he said dryly.

"Don't get me wrong. I like sex—but on my own terms. For me to really enjoy it, I need more than an athlete for a partner."

He smiled. "You're a throwback to another age, Miss Molly."

"So are you, O'Donnelly. Get your consciousness raised."

Dash raked his hair back from his face and looked away. "My God, you're not what I expected to find when I went looking for you today."

Molly tried to keep her chin up and her smile in place. Inside, she was churning and not nearly as brave as she pretended. Had she only known him a few hours? It seemed much longer than that.

She said, "Will you let me take the colt to my place?"

His head snapped up again. "No. He stays here."

"But—"

"He's a valuable animal, and we've got the proper security here. I'm sorry, Molly. I'm not the only villain in this case. The insurance company would refuse to let him leave our farm, too. You'll have to stay here. I'll have a room prepared in the house—"

"I can't stay in your house!"

"You want to pitch a tent in the front yard?"

"No, but—"

"And you can't run back and forth from your place several times a day. You'd be on the road two hours a day. You'll have to stay here." He grinned. "I promise you'll have your own room with an unbreakable lock on the door.''

Molly hesitated. Then she cast a glance into the fenced meadow and looked at the dark colt again. He had become bored with the people and was trotting purposefully up and down the fence, tossing his head and snorting into the wind.

He was magnificent, all right.

And Molly could reach him.

"All right," she said. "I'll do it."

Dash smiled broadly. "How much will it cost me?"

"Four thousand was your last offer, as I recall. For that, I'll have a saddle and a jockey on him. He'll be ready to race."

"Excellent. Shall we drive back to my office and put some of the details on paper?"

"A legal contract, you mean?"

"It's the wisest move, don't you think?"

"Forget it," Molly declared cheerfully, getting into the Jeep once more and slamming the door behind her. "I won't sign any contracts with the O'Donnelly name on them."

"For crying out loud, Molly!" Dash hurried around the Jeep and got in the driver's side. "Let's be reasonable."

"It's not negotiable," she said primly. "My father was screwed by yours because of a supposedly legal contract. I won't make the same mistake. A handshake will do."

Dash shook his head, more admiringly than in exasperation. "You're a stubborn woman, Miss Molly."

"But I'll get the job done," she vowed.

"I'm counting on it."

Dash started the Jeep. But from the back seat, Seabiscuit suddenly leaned forward and gave Dash's ear a huge, slobbery lick.

"He likes you," Molly said with a laugh. "He doesn't kiss just anybody, you know."

Dash sent her a smoldering look. "Neither do I."

Molly decided that remark needed no answer, even if she could make her vocal cords work, so she sat back in her seat and enjoyed the ride. The wind whipped her hair into a tangle, but she didn't care. It felt good.

She didn't delude herself, though. Dash's kiss had felt good. Wonderful, in fact. She'd never been so turned on by a man in her life.

But she'd kept her wits and was proud of it. She was assertive and independent, and she was glad she'd stopped Dash before the situation got out of control—without making him angry. He'd accepted her terms and she felt strong.

She suspected Dash was stronger, however. It was going to be a struggle working near him.

Arriving back at his office, they were greeted by a puzzling scene.

A large white limousine was parked in the middle of the drive, surrounded by half-a-dozen stern-faced men wearing dark suits and carrying walkie-talkies.

"Our visitors from the Middle East," Dash said. "They're— What the hell!"

On the hood of the elegant car sat three teenagers. One wore a traditional burnoose. The other two were typical American kids to Molly's eye—except they were armed with rifles. The dark-suited bodyguards watched them nervously.

"Damnation!" Dash jammed on the brakes, and the Jeep screeched to a stop.

At that moment the female teenager took aim with her weapon and pulled the trigger. Twenty feet away on a fence stood a line of crystal stemware, and as the bullet struck the first glass, it burst into a thousand pieces. The teenagers cheered.

Dash leapt from the vehicle and stormed toward the kids. Molly scrambled out and followed him. Belatedly she realized the rifles weren't rifles at all, but BB guns. As Dash arrived at the limousine, the boy in the white flowing robes accepted the gun offered by the girl, took aim and shot another wineglass off the nearby fence.

Dash thundered, "What's the meaning of this?"

The girl turned to him and blinked in the sunlight, smiling provocatively. She wore a crooked turban on her head, clearly a gift from the Middle Eastern boy, and she twirled the end of it seductively. "Hi ya, Dad. We're having some target practice."

She was pretty, petite and blond, but she had managed to disguise most of her attractive qualities by hacking her hair down to uneven clumps that had been slicked up to stand in enormous spikes that were tinted purple at the ends. Her pose on the hood of the car was like that of a starlet—legs crossed, shoulders flung back. She faced her father's wrath calmly.

"Are you crazy?" Dash demanded. "Somebody could get hurt!"

"Chill out, man," the other American boy said with disdain. He was chewing gum and wore an enormous T-shirt decorated with a huge pair of red lips and a lascivious-looking tongue. "Mom lets us shoot clay pigeons in Newport all the time."

"This isn't Newport," Dash snapped, swinging on the boy. "It's a horse farm with millions of dollars' worth of animals wandering around. If you blind one of them with your careless—"

"We're shooting at *glasses,* man," said the boy. Then he laughed.

"That's enough!" Dash roared. "Get off that car at once! Give me those guns! The two of you march up to your rooms this instant and stay there until—"

"But Grandad told us to entertain Ahmal, Dad," the girl protested, patting the foreign boy on his arm. "We're supposed to show him a good time, you know?"

"*You* show him a good time," St. John said to his sister. "Hey, man, who's the babe?"

Molly, having guessed she was the "babe" in question, stopped beside Dash and eyed the teenagers. "I'm Molly," she said.

"Good Golly," St. John cracked. "Hey, man, you sure can pick 'em, can't you?"

His jaw tense with anger, Dash said, "Molly, this is my son, St. John, and my daughter, Nicolette. They were *supposed* to be looking after their brother, Montgomery, this afternoon, but heaven only knows what's become of him."

"Chill," St. John said lazily. "Gummy's playing Nintendo."

Molly didn't like the rude stare of Dash's son, so she returned the look wattage for wattage and was rewarded when St. John turned pink around the ears and looked away. She said, "I'm sure these kids weren't doing any harm, Dash. They know all about firearms and safety, if they've used shotguns. And they'll be willing to clean up all the broken glass right away, I'm sure.''

Nikki's heavily mascaraed eyes popped wide and she began to nod. "Yeah, we'll clean it up. Right, Sinner? No harm done.''

"Do it immediately," Dash said. "Then find Montgomery. Ahmal can come with me.''

"But—"

"You have no choice in the matter, Nicolette.''

"What are we supposed to *do*?'' The girl wailed. "It's so *boring* around here! We can't go shopping and your cable channels stink. There's nothing going *on!*''

"Here.'' Dash dug into his pants pocket and came up with a wad of bills. "Take some money and go to the mall again. Julio will drive you.''

Nikki brightened. "Great! How much do I get?''

Dash looked stymied for a moment. "How much do you need?''

"Fifty bucks," St. John put in. "For dinner and video games.''

Nikki nodded. "Okay, fifty bucks.''

Clearly Dash hadn't the faintest idea how far fifty dollars might go with a couple of teenagers set loose in a shopping mall, for he handed the money over with the air of a desperate man. "Take it," he ordered, "and get out of here before you start any more trouble.''

St. John handed over his gun, then slid off the hood and put his hand out for Ahmal to slap. "Nice meetin' you, man. Come back again and I'll show you those magazines I was telling you about.''

"St. John!'' Dash said warningly.

St. John shrugged and walked away. Over his shoulder, he said to his father, "You got good taste in women, man, but you got no sense of humor."

Nikki winked at Ahmal and tossed him her turban. Flirtatiously she waved her fingertips at the startled young man before prancing after her brother.

Dash blew a sigh of exasperation. "Those kids," he said to Molly, "drive me up a wall."

Ahmal handed over his weapon, too, and looked politely confused. "Tell me what this means, drive you up a wall? I am trying to learn this language, and it is very difficult sometimes."

Molly laughed. "Never mind, Ahmal. Shall we go for a walk? I expect Mr. O'Donnelly has business to attend to."

Solemnly Ahmal said, "My father is here to buy a horse."

"Well, let's you and me go poking around the stables while they talk, shall we? Do you like horses?"

"Very much," the boy said warmly, climbing off the car.

"Thanks," Dash said, relief obvious in his face. "I'll go see his father and try to find someone else to conduct the tour. If you'll wait half an hour or so—"

"I will."

"Molly—"

"Shut up," she said, and grinned. "Just call it another favor."

He didn't have a chance to respond because an instant later, the office door banged back on its hinges, and a burly, white-haired man stepped out onto the porch. His voice was deep and powerful. "Good God!"

Dash looked around and muttered, "Oh, hell."

"Your father?" Molly inquired, then didn't wait for an answer. She cut around Dash and faced the old man as he stumped off the porch and strode toward her, looking murderous.

"Get off my land, you!" he shouted. "You're that Pym's—you're—good Lord!"

He shambled to a stop, looking surprised to see Molly standing bravely in his path, staunchly ready for a fistfight. "Bite my breeches," he said, blinking. "You look just like Margaret."

"She's my mother," Molly said harshly.

Dash closed his eyes and prayed for a bolt of lightning to strike—hoping it might blast them all off the face of the earth before the real explosions started. He should have known Dillon would be lurking around, hoping to be the one to order Paddy Pym's daughter off his land. Molly looked just as ready to do battle. She was bristling for a fight. It was *Clash of the Titans,* all right.

"Pop," Dash began, fearing for his father's health as Dillon's face began to turn purple.

"I can fight my own battles!" Dillon snarled, advancing on Molly like a marauding warrior.

"You're too old to fight any battles," Molly blazed, cocking her fists on her hips and sticking out her chin. "You're not much good for anything, are you, old man?"

"Shut your mouth, you—"

"You can't order me around!"

"By God, I'll take a whip to you!"

"Try it," Molly challenged, "and I'll break your arm!"

"Get me some soap," Dillon bellowed. "I'm going to wash out this girl's mouth!"

"You couldn't wrestle a kitten to the ground," she said, matching him decibel for decibel. "Stop threatening me, or I'll do some real damage!"

Towering over her, Dillon suddenly gave a short burst of laughter. "You're a little hothead, aren't you? Just like your mother."

Molly's face was dark and very tense. "I won't take any guff from the likes of you."

"You don't back off from a fight, either," Dillon said with a mixture of wonderment and annoyance. "Well, that's just like your old man. His stubborn streak got him into a lot of trouble, you know."

"Not as much trouble as *you* got him into," she retorted.

"Ah, he was just a foolish old Irishman who'd rather deal in black magic than common sense. I suppose that's why you're here, too? To charm that crazy horse of my son's?"

"My arrangement is with him, not you," Molly shot back. "I owe you nothing but a shot in the back, if I get the chance. Dash, give me one of those guns. Why, I'll—"

Dash barely managed to keep the BB guns out of Molly's grasp, and he found himself laughing at the scene they made—both furious and unforgiving, both poking their chins out like little kids in a playground standoff.

"Stop it, both of you," he said.

"She started it," Dillon began. "She insulted me—"

"*Stop it,* Pop. I mean it. I've hired Molly, and that's the end of it. You'll be civil to her, you understand?"

"He's too thickheaded to understand," Molly cracked.

"And you," Dash said, swinging on her, "will keep a lock on your tongue or I'll do something about it. Hear me?"

His gaze must have communicated exactly how he'd control her tongue, because Molly opened her mouth to protest, then thought twice and closed it again.

"That's better," Dash said. "Pop, I want you to see about the evening assignments in the stables. I'll go talk to the visitors. Molly, I'll see you shortly. We'll have dinner."

"You can't have dinner with her! These buyers expect your full attention!"

"Pop, button your lip or—"

"I'm not staying for dinner," Molly interrupted. "I'm going home."

"Going home?" Dash echoed, his plans for a long, cozy evening with her disappearing down the proverbial drain.

"I'll be back tomorrow," she said firmly. "As long as you promise to keep this old goat out of my way."

"Molly—"

"Let her go," Dillon advised. "Maybe she'll break her neck on the way home."

"Pop!"

Molly tossed her head and marched for her truck. On her heels, her three-legged dog hopped quickly to keep up with her. Dash watched her climb into the cab of her vehicle and gun the engine. With a fiery glance cast in his direction, she crashed the gears and roared out of the lane.

"By God," said Dillon beside him as they watched her go, "she's a fine-looking girl. It's too bad I'm going to have to kill her with me own hands."

"Pop," Dash said, barely hanging on to his patience. "Put a sock in it."

Five

Molly wished she could turn her back on Dash O'Donnelly and his damned beautiful horse. His father was a colossal pain in the neck and he was going to be hard to keep in hand.

But the mortgage payment was due again, and a girl had to eat now and then. So she didn't have much of a choice.

She telephoned her mother in Florida for advice.

"Who?" Margaret Pym asked. "Dillon O'Donnelly? Is he still alive? What an impossible man!"

"He remembers you pretty fondly, Mom."

"Does he? Oh, he carried a torch forever!"

"A torch? What d'you mean, Mom?"

"This phone call's costing you a fortune, dear. I'm sure you can't possibly be interested—"

"Is there some history between you and O'Donnelly?"

"Only in his imagination, I'm sure."

"But—"

"Molly," her mother said more seriously, "he's a terrible bully and wants everything he sees. He was always jealous of your father—"

"Because of you?"

"I don't know," she said evasively. "Maybe. Years ago, when I wouldn't give him the time of day, he set out to punish your father. But that was ancient history. Surely he's happy now."

"That's not my impression."

"Well, tell me how it all turns out, darling. I've got a bridge game tonight, so I must run."

Molly was glad that her mother was so busy and happy living in Florida. She shared a pleasant condominium with a friend from her youth and spent her time playing cards and baking. From time to time, Margaret also visited the racetracks.

With affection, Molly said, "Okay. 'Night, Mom. I love you."

"I love you, too, Molly. Don't work too hard. That old farm isn't worth all the heartache, you know."

Molly didn't disagree, but she wanted to.

It was still misty the next morning when Molly returned to O'Donnelly Farms in her rattling pickup truck.

She pulled into a parking space beside the office building, then got out. Seabiscuit jumped out beside her and made a beeline for a patch of sunlight on the porch steps. He lay down with a gusty sigh and went to sleep. Molly looked at him and wished she could be as relaxed as he was.

With her heart set on getting the job done and going home as soon as possible, without getting into any trouble, Molly got busy unfastening the tarp on the bed of her truck.

That was when Dash showed up. Molly heard the clatter of steel-shod hooves on pavement and turned in time to see a long-legged bay horse appear out of the mist. Dash rode with the ease of a man long accustomed to the saddle. He'd been a champion polo player at the local matches, and he looked handsomer than any human had a right to look.

In jeans and a faded red sweater over an open-necked shirt, he sat lightly in the saddle with his boot-clad legs clinging to the sleek sides of his mount. The two of them looked well-bred and confident. Dash was the boss man surveying his property, and he didn't look terribly delighted by what he'd seen so far.

Just setting her eyes on him again made Molly's heart beat faster.

She cursed her heart and wished to hell she could control the way she felt about Dash.

He saw Molly then, and his expression lightened. He reined his horse in her direction. Formal but sardonic, he said, "Good morning, Miss Molly."

How did he manage to sound threatening and teasing at the same time? Molly didn't dare meet his eyes and tried to keep her voice gruff. "Good morning, O'Donnelly."

He halted the horse just two paces from where she stood, and leaned down to pat the animal's neck. "I thought we progressed to first names yesterday."

Molly stole a glance up at him. "Hello, Dash."

"Much better," he commended with a flicker of a smile. His black hair had been ruffled by his ride, and a flush of exertion shone on his cheeks. He crossed one leg over the pommel of his saddle and leaned on it easily to watch her work. "You look charming this morning."

Molly had deliberately dressed in an unflattering flannel shirt and pulled her hair into a ponytail, so she didn't feel especially charming. To him, she said, "You look beat."

"Thanks."

He *did* look tired, but something besides lack of sleep was bothering him. With a burst of intuition, Molly asked, "Did your visitors buy your horse yesterday?"

"No," he said shortly. "They found one they liked better elsewhere."

"Oh, sorry." Molly noticed the lines of tension around his mouth and wondered if he had more than unsold horses on his mind.

Then Dash met her gaze, and his grouchiness seemed to fade. He asked, "Did you dream about me last night, Miss Molly?"

How had he guessed? Molly fought down a blush and turned to yank at the cord on the tarp. "I was busy last night, getting ready for today."

"You're going to start right away?"

"That's what you want, isn't it?"

"Yes, I need Mashed Potato under saddle as soon as possible."

Need. Molly heard the word and wondered if Dash hadn't told her everything. "Well, I'm here and ready to go. I started your man working at my place and came right over."

"Do you think your farm will survive without you?"

"I suppose. The old guy you sent over seems quite competent."

"He's the best we have. You have to get up pretty early to fool Tommy."

Molly said, "It looks like you're an early bird this morning, too."

"Working," he said, with a gesture that took in the whole farm and all the responsibilities that went along with it. "My father takes the three-year-olds out at five every morning, and I've started going along. I find I like seeing the sun rise."

"Oh?"

Molly had a lot on her mind and she decided to get the worst over with. "Look," she said, "I'm sorry for what happened yesterday. With you, first of all. And with your father."

Dash's brows rose. "You're apologizing for yelling at my father?"

"No," Molly corrected, "I *meant* to yell at him. I just didn't mean to call him names. He deserves them, of course, but my behavior was—well, it was beneath me."

"I see," Dash said, leaning on his elbow and looking amused at last. "Should I submit you to a body search?"

"To make sure I'm not carrying any lethal weapons?"

Dash smiled. "He may be a tremendous pain, but he's my father, after all. I can't stand around and watch while you murder him."

Molly couldn't hold back a small smile of triumph. "He's fearing for his life, I hope."

"Actually, I think he's looking forward to seeing you today."

"You're kidding!"

"Not at all. Do you know, that fight the two of you had yesterday seems to have cleared out his arteries or something. He's a new man this morning."

Molly feigned annoyance. "Damn!"

Dash laughed, and it relaxed his face, making him look much more approachable. "If I didn't know better, I'd think you were actually good for him. He hasn't been himself since your father passed away. I wonder if that old feud hasn't kept him alive and kicking all these years?"

"Do you mean to say, if I'm nice to him, he actually might take sick?"

"Anything's possible."

Molly gave the idea some thought and shook her head. "I can't do it. I can't be nice to him."

"How about me?" Dash asked, sounding husky suddenly. "You said you were sorry about what happened with me, too. I hope you're not serious."

"I am." Idly, she extended her hand to Dash's horse, and it immediately shoved its velvety muzzle into her palm to snuffle her. Slowly Molly said, "I didn't mean to let things get as far as they did. It never should have happened."

"The kissing, you mean?"

"And—and the rest of it." Molly didn't want to catalog her sins of yesterday. She deeply regretted allowing Dash to touch her and getting so carried away. Mainly she'd been shaken up by the ease with which he'd overwhelmed her, and she didn't want a repeat performance. She let his horse lick her palm for salt and stole a look up at Dash.

"I see," he said solemnly, reading the thoughts on her face. "But I'm afraid I don't agree."

"Well, this isn't your decision to make," she replied airily. By habit, Molly took the horse's head in her hands and cradled it, allowing the animal to rub his face against her shirt. She used the horse's actions to avoid looking up at Dash. Trying to remember the speech she'd carefully practiced in the truck on the way over, she said, "I thought about us last night—"

"So did I," he interrupted. "I was up half the night."

"That's not what I meant."

"I woke up ready for you, in fact," Dash said quietly. "For a second, I thought you were with me in my bed. I reached for you—"

"Please," Molly said hurriedly. Inside, she was suddenly quivering. "I—I don't want to get carried away again."

"Why not?"

"Because, damn it! You're you and I'm me."

"And we're attracted to each other."

Molly hurriedly wiped her face clean. "I'll work for you," she said harshly, "but I can't have an affair with you."

"You're afraid, aren't you?"

"No, but—"

"It's not me you're afraid of. It's yourself."

"I'm not afraid of anything!"

"No?"

"No!"

He put his hand down. "Then you won't be afraid to come with me right now. Jump up and I'll take you over to the East Barn. We'll get you a horse and we'll go for a ride this morning."

The idea appalled Molly. Alone together, they'd be explosive, she was sure. "I—I have work to do. I want to get started."

"I know you do, but there are some things we need to settle first. About Mashed Potato. And us. Come on. Give me your hand."

"I don't want to ride with you."

"You're afraid."

"No, I'm—I just—"

"Come on."

"Dash—"

"*Come,*" he commanded, and there was something about his tone Molly couldn't disobey.

As if mesmerized, she reached for his hand, and when he kicked his own boot out of the stirrup, she put her foot into it and vaulted up onto the horse. But at the last second, Dash grabbed Molly's hips and twisted her so that she ended up sitting sideways on the pommel, across his thighs.

"Wait a minute," she objected, squirming.

"Too late." Dash had one arm around her, and with the other hand, he gathered up the reins. "Relax, Miss Molly. Why, you're tense as a rabbit at a dog show."

Valiantly Molly tried to avoid any body contact, but it was impossible. For starters, they bumped heads. And sitting on his lap brought a hot blush to her face. She could feel the strength in his thighs, and the pressure of her shoulder in his chest kept her balanced as the horse picked up his feet and began to move off. "I can walk, you know. This horse is too skittish for two of us."

"Junket is about as skittish as a jersey cow. He's seventeen years old, and my youngest son rides him. It's you who's upset this morning."

"I'm just trying to keep my perspective."

Dash laughed, and Molly could feel the vibration in his chest. He demanded, "What does that mean?"

He squeezed his legs and the horse settled into an easy, head-bobbing walk. Molly had no choice but to grab for support. Trouble was, there was nothing to hold on to. She ended up slipping her hand through Dash's belt. She cleared her throat and said, "It means I want to keep my attention focused on my job. We settled this yesterday. I can't train your colt properly if I—if we—well, it's too complicated, that's all."

"I don't think it's complicated at all. You're a single woman, and I've been divorced for years. We're both unentangled at the moment."

She frowned, wondering how he knew there was no man in her life at the moment. Was it so obvious? "I've had boyfriends, you know. Several."

"Boy friends," Dash said. "That's different. I'm no boy, and I don't want to be your friend. In the platonic sense, that is."

"You've made no secret about what you want!"

"I don't believe in beating around the bush, not when I'm struck by a woman the way I'm struck by you."

Under her breath, Molly muttered, "I'd like to strike you, all right."

He laughed. "If that's your pleasure, we can do that later, but I'd rather try a more traditional first encounter, if you don't mind."

Blushing again, she said, "You're bold!"

"And you're not as innocent as you're pretending this morning."

"I never said I was innocent. I'm just not interested."

"Liar," he whispered in her ear.

Molly was glad she didn't have to look into his eyes and kept her head straight ahead. "I told you yesterday. I hate the idea of a quick, stupid affair."

"Me, too." He shifted her weight to be more comfortable. "I like long, long affairs with women who are smart and responsive and sexually alive. Like you, Miss Molly."

"I am not responsive or—or sexually alive, either!"

"You don't think so? Hold the reins."

"What? Dash, wait—"

But he forced the reins into Molly's hands, and suddenly she was guiding their horse down the lane. "Close your eyes," he said. "Junket will find his own way back to the barn if he has to. All you have to do is sit still."

"But—"

"Close your eyes."

Though she was quite warm, Molly shivered. The morning mist was still rising softly from the cool ground, cloaking them from the rest of the world. The tree branches on either side of the lane seemed to grow out of the fog, stretching their fragrant branches up into the clouds. Only the slow cadence of Junket's steps broke the stillness. It was a magically beautiful morning, really. A morning full of strange excitement.

"Do it," he whispered.

"Dash, stop."

He laughed, sounding slightly breathless against her ear. "You don't even know what I'm going to do yet. Close your eyes, damn you."

She held her breath as Dash tightened his arm around her and with the other hand began to draw aimless patterns on her legs. She was powerless to stop him, for she gripped his belt with one hand and controlled the steadily walking horse with the other. But Dash's touch warmed Molly, and she trembled involuntarily. To avoid seeing her own response to him, she closed her eyes at last.

"Good girl. Now tell me what you see."

"Wh—what?"

He continued to caress the tops of her thighs in a slow, delicious trailing of his fingertips. His featherlight touch induced a rush of heat to Molly's lower limbs. When she clamped her knees tightly together, he said, "Tell me what's on your mind right now."

"Why are you doing this?"

"To prove a point. Tell me what you're thinking."

"How can I think when you're doing that?"

"That's the point. How do I make you feel?"

"Nervous. I don't trust you."

As if understanding that her legs were already fully aroused, Dash slipped his caress up her thigh and began to make slow, wonderful circles on Molly's stomach. His hand was large, but sensitive, automatically avoiding her ticklish spot, but homing in on the place where Molly's whole bloodstream suddenly seemed to be concentrated beneath the surface. At the same time, he began to nuzzle Molly's ear with his nose. "I won't hurt you," he murmured. "I promise. I won't do anything if you tell me to stop."

She bit back a noise. "I still don't trust you."

"Because of the past? The thing between our fathers?"

Molly squeezed her eyes tighter, aware of the sensual motion of the horse beneath her—motion that seemed to amplify the unmistakable message radiating from Dash's lower body. Sitting so awkwardly in his lap, cradled in his embrace, she began to imagine they were engaged in a very different kind of rhythmic activity. Her breath began to come faster.

Eyes still closed, she managed to say, "You're just not the trustworthy type."

He laughed softly. "I like that, I think. What are you feeling now?"

"You're unfastening my shirt."

She should have stopped him. If he was trying to make a point, Molly had forgotten what it was. All she knew was that he could make her feel scared and wonderful at the same time.

His fingers were agile with the buttons and in a moment, a breath of refreshing cool air struck Molly in the chest. Beneath the flannel, Dash discovered a second shirt, a cotton tank top Molly wore instead of a bra. It was securely tucked into her jeans, and she was relieved that he wouldn't be able to pull it up without considerable wrestling.

But Dash wasn't interested in stripping her of the tank top. Not yet. He began to draw languid circles around her breasts, never quite touching them, but somehow sending tingles directly to her nipples. They grew hard instantly, and Molly clamped down on an exclamation.

"Say it," Dash coaxed, starting to nibble on the length of her throat. "Tell me what you feel."

Molly leaned her head back so that he could begin to press warm kisses along her neck. In an unsteady whisper, she said, "That feels—it's very—um—nice."

"Nice?" he echoed, laughing. "My dear Miss Molly, I'm many things, but not nice. Am I making you feel hot inside?"

"I guess so."

"Where?"

It was delicious, really. Rocking along on the horse, enjoying those wonderful caresses, listening to that hypnotic voice.

"Everywhere," she breathed.

"Here?" he asked, touching her breast at last, and rubbing the hard nipple with his palm until Molly released a soft gasp. "And the other one, too?"

"Dash—"

"Where should I touch you next, Molly?"

She wanted to open her legs and let him find the spot that ached so desperately for his touch.

"Molly?"

"I—I can't say it. Oooh, why do I break all the rules with you?"

"Maybe," Dash said, kissing her throat and discovering the way her pulse hammered with excitement, "it's time to change the rules."

"You make me crazy, Dash."

"It's quite mutual, Miss Molly. Can you feel how much I'm attracted to you?"

She *could* feel the physical evidence of his attraction. "This is foolish."

"But fun, right?"

"We can't finish what you're starting, Dash."

"I've never tried making out on a horse," he admitted. "I can think of too many better places, actually. Are you going to touch me?"

Molly's hand remained locked on his belt. He had continued to stimulate her breasts—slowly, gently—

and Molly's blood felt thick and tingly in her veins. "If I touch you," she said, "we'll go too far."

"How far is too far?"

"I've already let you go beyond the limit," she murmured, languidly enjoying his caresses and finally forcing her eyes open. She looked deeply into Dash's smiling gaze and wondered dimly if she could hold out much longer.

"Then a little farther won't matter. Touch me."

Instead of complying with his wishes, she risked her balance to brush his hand away. "No, I'm here to work, not for slap and tickle."

Dash laughed. He loved the way Molly responded to him. He'd never known a woman so meant for his lovemaking. It was just damned frustrating that she was trapped in the same body with a brain that was so stubborn.

"Let me down," she said, turning prickly when they reached the East Barn. "I won't ride with you anymore."

Because they were within view of some of the farm employees, Dash obeyed and slung Molly to the ground. She landed lightly, and he was pleased to see a bright stain of pink beneath her golden suntan as she hastily buttoned her shirt.

He liked her sensible side, despite the fervor she had for keeping it under control. But he also liked the fierce pride that showed in her every move, her every glance. Despite her youth, Molly was a woman who refused to become a meaningless sexual encounter. She had strong ideas and an iron will to go with them.

He wanted to know her better.

"We'll find you a horse," he said, and took her into the stable where the farm's riding horses were kept. "I'll show you around the place."

He spent the morning with Molly, riding her around O'Donnelly Farms and taking pleasure in showing her his father's empire. It pained Dash to think he and his father were on the verge of losing the place, but he had begun to wonder if the huge, privately owned racing stables weren't already a thing of the past. He hated the thought of selling out to a syndicate of investors, but the weight of debt had grown so large that he doubted he could dig a way out and still save the family company.

Unless Mashed Potato was as good as Dash prayed he was.

Dash considered asking Molly what she thought, but she ended up volunteering her ideas. She, too, was saddened by the impersonal, corporate feel to racing. But she offered no means of escape.

Dash insisted Molly have lunch at the house with him. After a short argument, she agreed. Dash suspected she was very hungry. They rode over to the house and tethered their horses in the shade of twin maples. They ate on the veranda, a vantage point from where they could see Mashed Potato gallop around his meadow.

Molly quickly demolished the sandwich that Patreen O'Shay, the family cook since Dash was a boy, brought on a tray with iced tea, cucumber salad and thin slices of lemon meringue pie. Patreen gave Molly a good looking-over, then shot Dash a meaningful look and a swift nod before departing for the kitchen. Molly didn't notice Patreen's silent approval, but instead ate voraciously and asked questions about the colt.

"I wasn't here when he was born," Dash told her when he was asked. "I don't know how he was treated those first few weeks, but I'm sure he was well taken care of."

"You never know," Molly said doubtfully. "What happened to his mother?"

"She lived through the summer, then died in October of colic. She'd been prone to that all her life."

"He was hand-raised after that, or with a surrogate mother?"

"Hand-raised. He rejected all other mares. I suppose he missed his mama."

"Was Mashed Potato her first foal?"

"Sixth. But her first with Scalloped."

Molly nodded, watching the colt intently from her chair and chewing her mouthful of cucumber without thinking. She asked more questions, and Dash answered them as best he could. Some of the things she wanted to know were beyond him—like how many apples Mashed Potato had eaten during the winter.

"I think I'll go see him now," Molly said, getting up before Dash had finished his first bite of lemon meringue. "I want to talk to him."

Dash wanted to go along. He enjoyed watching Mashed Potato, and he was damned curious about exactly how Molly was going to start settling him down.

But he needed to spend a couple of hours crunching numbers on the computer in his office, and even the pleasure of Molly Pym's company couldn't keep him from that duty.

So Dash made his excuses and sent Molly on her way. When last he saw her, she was climbing onto the fence enclosing Mashed Potato's meadow.

Molly didn't see Dash again that day. She sat and talked to Mashed Potato for the afternoon. Nothing more, just talk. She wanted him to smell her and get used to her voice. She made no move to get close to him. Patience.

Around five o'clock, Dillon O'Donnelly appeared behind the wheel of the family Jeep. He braked to a stop, raising a cloud of dust that sent Mashed Potato charging for the shelter of the trees.

Dillon got out of the Jeep, looking thunderous. "Just what the hell are you doing here? Trespassing?"

Molly faced him with all the hostility she'd learned at her father's knee. "Don't try bullying me, you old goat."

"I won't have you tormenting my animal!"

"This one isn't yours," Molly returned, refusing to budge when Dillon blustered up to her. "Your son hired me to work with him."

Dillon's face was very red. "My son has some pretty foolish ideas, and this one's the worst! The idiot ought to try thinking with his brains, not his pants!"

"Keep your voice down," Molly snapped, finding herself annoyed that Dillon felt free to criticize his own son. "You're upsetting the colt."

"Upsetting the—?" Dillon sputtered, "Why, you little—"

"Stop spouting off and be useful," she interrupted. "If you're going to hang around, the least you can do is answer a few questions."

Dillon's eyes popped wide, and Molly realized they were dark gray, just the color of Dash's. The knowledge gave her a moment's hesitation. Then he said, "You can't order me around, young lady."

"Just tell me about this colt's mother, and stop yakking."

Dillon frowned. "What about his mother?"

"Did she have any unusual traits? Had she been raced? Was she a nurturing mother or—"

"She was a damn good mare," Dillon said. "We raced her for three years, then she came here and produced some fine foals. This one's just crazy, that's all."

"Was Scalloped?"

"Crazy? Of course not." Dillon stumped forward and placed his forearms on the top rail of the fence so he could watch the colt snorting as he dug up the loose earth with his hooves. Getting misty around the eyes, Dillon said, "Scalloped was the best horse I've ever trained. He was fast on the track and a perfect gentleman in the barn. Why, he used to follow Dash around like a puppy dog."

"What?"

"Scalloped was Dash's pet. His mother died a few weeks after he was born, and Dash took him, fed him from a bottle and treated him just like his own baby."

Molly had a hard time picturing Dash in the role of nursemaid. "You're kidding, right?"

"Hell, no." Dillon allowed a grudging grin. "That was around the time his own son was born, but Dash spent his time right here at the farm, looking after that colt."

"Wait a minute, you mean Dash—"

"Sure," Dillon went on as if Molly wasn't there. "He babied Scalloped and taught him tricks like a circus pony, put his first saddle on him. Nobody was more proud than Dash when he won at Churchill Downs."

Dillon rhapsodized a little longer, but Molly stopped listening. She wondered why Dash had seen fit to treat an animal with more love than his own child.

She cut across Dillon's monologue. "Why wasn't Dash with his own family?"

"What?" Dillon looked vague. "Oh, that wife of his—she knew what she wanted, and Dash didn't fit into the picture. He didn't drink tea with his pinky stuck up in the air, you know?"

"His ex-wife is—?"

"A Daddy's girl." Dillon shrugged, dismissing the woman. "A good-looker, and rich as Midas, but she needed a carriage horse for a husband, not a wild young buck with a mind of his own like Dash. Oh, he tried to patch things up with her—against my advice. He went back to her twice." Dillon winked. "Two more kids, right?"

"Hmm," said Molly.

"But she threw him out every time, so he started climbing mountains and all. Now he's back where he belongs."

"Does he belong here?"

"Sure. Nobody loves this place the way Dash does. Except myself, you understand. But he's got it in his blood, and it'll all belong to him someday."

"Soon, I hope," Molly said dryly.

Dillon looked at her and laughed. "You don't like me much, do you, young lady?"

"Nope."

"Because of Paddy."

"I don't even like hearing you say his name."

Dillon leveled his finger at Molly. "I didn't do a blessed thing to that fool father of yours. He made all the wrong choices on his own. Give him two choices, and he'd always pick the wrong one. Except once."

"Oh? What was that?"

"Your ma," Dillon said succinctly. And then and there, his eyes began to well with tears, and he said, "Your ma was the best thing that ever happened to Paddy Pym."

"What do you know about it?" Molly demanded.

"I know everything, young lady. Except where she is now."

"You think I'd tell you?"

He laughed bitterly. "I half hoped she'd tell me herself. But she didn't. I guess I know what that means, don't I?"

"You haven't gone to see her," Molly pointed out.

He snorted. "What kind of man does that? If she wanted me, she knew where to find me."

"She didn't want you."

"Never did, I guess," Dillon acknowledged. "Funny, huh? Most of the things I did all my life, I did for Maggie."

Emotion finally overcame Molly. "Don't you talk like that," she cried. "I don't want to hear you say her name! Do you know what pain you gave all of us?"

"Hey—"

"Go away! Just get away from here before I—before I take your stupid neck and—"

"I'm going, I'm going," Dillon snapped. And he went.

Six

___

Molly walked back to the O'Donnelly house later when her stomach began to growl. She was greeted at the door by Patreen O'Shay, the housekeeper. She was a small round woman with snowy white hair parted down the middle and separated into two buns over her ears. Her speech was ever so slightly tinged with an Irish lilt.

"Why, you'll be wanting a bath before dinner, won't you, dear?" Patreen said kindly. "Just leave your boots here by the door, and I'll show you a room. Dash had your things sent over this afternoon. I hope that's fine with you."

Molly sat down in a rickety chair by the door, obviously positioned there so that nobody ventured into the house with dirty boots. She left hers in a heap with footwear of every size and configuration imaginable, then followed Patreen up the wide, winding staircase, which looked like a set for *Gone With the Wind*.

"This is quite a place," Molly remarked, glancing at the portraits hanging in the hall as she strolled along an oriental carpet in her sock feet.

"Oh, it's fixed up real fine now," Patreen acknowledged, bustling along the second-floor corridor. "The house was built by Mr. Dillon's father, Sean O'Donnelly, who was a notorious gambler. He lost his fortune on a single horse race, but his creditors allowed him to keep the house—without the furniture. When Mr. Dillon inherited the place and started winning races with his horses, he bought back some of the original things—paintings of his relatives, mostly, and some of the furniture. But we've got whole rooms that are still empty! Why, here's a picture of Mr. Dillon's mama. Quite a woman, don't you think?"

The painting in question depicted a voluptuous, dark-eyed beauty reclining on a tumble of satin bedclothes, with her bosom proudly displayed and her black hair running riot over the pillows. It was the kind of picture Molly imagined hanging in a wild West saloon.

"Uh, yes, quite a woman," she said politely.

Patreen laughed. "The way Mr. Dillon tells it, his mama was a theatrical lady that Mr. Sean met in Ireland and brought back as his wife, but nobody was ever sure they really married."

"Oh?"

With a laugh, Patreen said, "She was a wicked one, too. Threw plates when her temper was high and slid down the bannisters in her underclothes every Christmas morning. Why, she sang for President Roosevelt once when he was visiting Saratoga, and rumor had it they were alone for *two hours!* After that, she got a dozen red roses every year on her birthday and never said who they came from. But we all suspect it was the President himself.''

"She was a real character."

"Yep. She died before Mr. Sean lost his money—had too much to drink and broke her neck diving into the swimming pool out back."

"Good heavens."

"Yes, but better to die quick like that than live in poverty, I suppose. She'd have hated that." Patreen turned left down a long hallway, unaware that Molly's background might be something other than privileged. "Then Mr. Dillon went off to the war and brought home a girl just as full of life as his mama. Margot was French, and she lived fast and died young, too. Dash was only ten when she was killed in a car accident—wrapped her convertible around a tree right here on the farm."

Molly thought of a ten-year-old Dash and felt a lump in her throat. "How sad," she murmured.

"They say she was going to meet a lover, since Mr. Dillon never really cared about her. I don't know about that. He's not one for telling people how he feels. Anyway, that's when I came to O'Donnelly Farms. I'm a cousin, you see, and I took care of Dash. My land, I'm chewing your ear off, aren't I?"

Without waiting for Molly's response, Patreen opened a bedroom door and led the way inside. "Will this room suit you, miss?"

Molly faltered in the doorway and for a moment she forgot the sad story of Dash's family. She admired the pretty pink-and-white room, decorated with white furniture and a pale pink carpet. The white, gauzy curtains were open on a pair of very tall French windows leading onto a second-story porch. It was a very feminine room decorated expertly and expensively, hardly what Molly expected in a house owned by two grown men whose priorities seemed to be horses, not women.

"It's lovely."

The older woman stood back, hands clasped and smiling, while Molly hesitantly admired her room. "Oh, it's lovely, all right," the housekeeper chatted. "Dash's wife had it fixed up when she came for a visit one summer—even paid for the renovations herself. I think you'll find it comfortable. The bath's through this door."

Molly followed and found herself in a spacious bathroom with a huge white circular tub and a marble sink, all surrounded by huge mirrors that managed to reflect both women from various angles. A stack of fluffy pink-and-white striped towels had been thoughtfully left on the countertop, which looked long enough to serve a buffet for a hundred people. Molly could imagine the expensive cosmetics Dash's high-society wife must have spread along that polished surface.

"It's very nice," Molly murmured, wondering how soon she could be soaking in a tub full of hot water and daydreaming about being rich and pampered.

"That other door leads to the bathroom on the other side." Patreen pointed to the door between the huge mirrors. "The two bathrooms connect so that Dash and his wife could visit now and then. They weren't totally separated, if I am any judge of human nature! Dash's room is through there, but I doubt you'll hear him. You can lock the door from either side, of course. Here, I'll do it myself."

"Thanks," Molly said as Patreen fastened the bolt. "It's nice of you to take such good care of me, Mrs. O'Shay. I thought I'd be more of an employee, not a guest."

Patreen seemed pleased. "You're a very welcome guest, no matter what you might hear from Mr. Dillon. We need a winner so badly, but I'm sure Dash has told you all that."

Molly decided it was safer not to answer, though her curiosity was piqued. She hesitated, but Patreen didn't seem to notice. The housekeeper kept talking at high speed.

"Dinner's in an hour," she told Molly. "If you're hungry, I've left some fruit in the bowl by the bed. If you want something else, come down to the kitchen yourself anytime. I only ask that you don't leave dirty dishes around the house."

"I'll be careful."

Patreen smiled. "Have a bath, then. Everybody does before dinner at this house—nobody's going to smell like stables at my table! But don't think you've got to get dressed up tonight. It's jeans and sweatshirts around here when we don't have business guests."

"Thanks."

In a minute, Molly was alone in her new quarters. She stripped off her clothes while running water into the tub. It came out in a steaming cloud, and after a short search, Molly found a selection of bath crystals in a glass jar. She sprinkled some into the water, then inhaled the sweet perfume that rose up from the tub. The mirrors reflected Molly's lean body.

Naked at last, she shook out her hair and slid into the silky water to relax. After riding all morning with Dash, she was glad to rest her muscles.

Eyes closed, she began to review all the things she'd learned about the O'Donnelly family. After hearing Patreen's tale, Molly decided she understood Dash better. He must have inherited a lot of characteristics from a long line of adventurous relatives. And the way he kept his feelings to himself no doubt stemmed from living in a family that valued flamboyant personality over genuine emotions and love. His grandmother had been a saloon singer, his grandfather a gambler. His own father had married the wrong woman, and she'd died young and neglected.

And Dash? Perhaps Molly knew why he'd spent his younger days roaming the earth in search of adventure. It was probably easier than staying at home and fighting to keep his family together.

It seemed that the O'Donnelly men had a penchant for marrying the wrong women, too. And Dash had been no exception to that rule.

A door slammed nearby, and Molly heard a whistle.

Dismayed, she sank down in the bubble bath. It was Dash, no mistake.

He was whistling something fast and Irish, and he slammed into his bathroom, just on the other side of the door from where Molly soaked in the tub. Hastily she reached for a towel. But her hand accidentally struck a bottle of shampoo, and it fell to the floor with a clatter.

"Molly?" Dash asked from the other side of the door.

She held her breath and considered not answering. But the door was locked—she'd seen Patreen do it herself—so there was no sense being afraid of him.

She cleared her throat awkwardly. "Yes, it's me."

Dash gave a delighted laugh. "Are you in the tub?"

Her face felt hot, as if he'd stared right through the door. "No, of course not!"

But he laughed again. "You are, aren't you?"

Appalled, Molly groaned. "Can't a girl have a few minutes to herself?"

"I'll bet you look beautiful."

She sank down until her chin touched the bubbles. "Please don't start anything, Dash!"

Her own reflection did look surprisingly pretty, however. Molly stared at the wide-eyed young woman in the gigantic mirrors around the tub and decided she didn't look like a rough horsewoman at the moment. She looked rich and pampered. And surprisingly sexy.

"Tell me," said Dash, with a tease in his voice. "Did you find any bubble bath?"

"Y—yes."

"The pink stuff? I love that. Doesn't it smell like a harem girl's?

"You're not getting an invitation to join me, so don't waste your breath, please."

"I can fantasize, can't I?"

Dash listened to the frustrated sigh that reached him through the closed bathroom door. He could picture Molly sitting bolt upright in the big white bathtub, surrounded by a cotton-candy fluff of bubbles, a woman interrupted during a pleasant bath. But surely the warm water had eased her tensions. Surely she looked lazy and lovely as she reclined against the side of the tub once more, convinced of her safety.

He leaned against the door and said persuasively, "I could come in and scrub your back."

"I know what else you'd like to scrub," she returned.

"Have a heart," Dash coaxed, laughing. "Give me something to dream about. Are you completely naked?"

"Dash—"

"Tell me," he begged. "I won't come in, I promise. The door's locked, right?"

"Right." She was silent for a moment, then said, "All right, yes, I'm naked."

"And your hair? Is it pinned up? Or—"

"I'm not telling you another thing," she said. Then, softer, "Unless you're naked, too."

Dash grinned. "Miss Molly! What an improper suggestion!"

Her voice sounded stronger. "You've been nothing but improper since we met. Undress, O'Donnelly."

He considered the idea, amused and growing more interested by the moment. "This could be the ultimate in safe sex, don't you think?"

"It gives new meaning to the phrase 'behind closed doors,' at least."

"You said yesterday you only liked sex on your own terms. Is this what you meant?"

"It's a poor second choice," she said, sounding amused. "But it'll have to do, won't it?"

"Unless you unlock this door."

"Take your clothes off, Dash."

The note of seduction in her voice was too much to resist. Dash began to unfasten the buttons on his shirt. He didn't have much experience with take-charge

women. It just surprised the hell out of him that Molly
could be so bold, but he decided he liked it.

Her voice came through the door again, more com-
manding this time. "Tell me what you're doing," she
ordered. "Every step, please."

He suppressed a laugh. "I'm unbuttoning my shirt.
There, now I'm taking it off." He threw it on the floor
and found himself enjoying the game.

"Are you wearing a belt?" she asked.

"It's coming off now."

"Shoes?"

"I left my boots downstairs."

"Then socks go next," she said with even more au-
thority. "Can you see yourself in the mirror, Dash?"

He could. And the gleam of anticipation was unmistakable in his eyes. Dash noticed his face had been
windburned sometime during the day—or was that
some kind of sexual flush? He tore off his socks.

Then Molly said, "Your jeans next, Dash. Do it
slowly, though."

It was a striptease played to an invisible audience,
but Dash found the whole experience delicious. In
fact, he was already breathing heavily as he jerked off
his jeans and skimmed his briefs down his hips. At
last, he stood in the bathroom with his discarded
clothes at his feet and his body looking rampant and
excited in the mirror. A fine sheen of perspiration had
begun to shine on his chest.

"Is everything off?"

"There's not a stitch on this body."

"You have a very nice body, Dash."

"How can you tell? You can't see it!"

"I'd rather concentrate on the inner you."

Dash wasn't sure he heard right. "The what?"

"Tell me a secret," she said.

"What kind of secret?"

"I want to know you better. I want to know what's under your skin."

Intimacy. That's what she wanted. Dash was at a loss. Suddenly he didn't know what to say.

"Dash?"

"I'm here."

"Is this too hard?"

"No," he said uncertainly. "It's just different."

"Tell me about your favorite teacher."

He started to laugh. "Molly, please don't make me talk about Sister Bernadette when I'm standing here with my—"

"Okay, okay. Tell me a dream."

Aha. That was more like it. "I dreamed about you last night. I dreamed we were—"

"No, no, not a sexy dream. Maybe one you've had more than once. One that bugs you."

"Oh, *that* dream."

"You have one?"

He turned around and leaned against the door. "Sure. I'm drowning."

"Tell me," she coaxed.

Dash had never been good at intimacy—giving women a part of himself. It had always been too hard. And too pointless. But Molly's gentle voice urged him on. And—oddly enough—standing there with no clothes on seemed to make things simpler. He said, "All right. I dream about the pool. Have you seen it?"

"The one out back? Yes, it's very pretty."

"In my dream, I fall off the diving board and I can't get out of the water. The sides of the pool are too high and I can't grab anything. I have to swim."

"Do you get tired?"

"Really tired." Even as he recalled his nightmare, his chest felt tight, his muscles heavy. "I swim until I can't move anymore. Then I start to yell—not for help, but out of frustration."

"Why don't you yell for help?"

"Because nobody will come, I guess. Sometimes..."

"Yes?"

"Sometimes I wake myself up," he admitted. "My grandmother, you know, drowned in the pool."

A long silence happened then. Dash closed his eyes and thought about his dream, wondering. He'd never been afraid of water. Never knew his grandmother, either. It felt weird to be saying these things to a stranger—things he didn't understand.

Almost too softly to hear, Molly said, "Sometimes I dream about riding a horse I can't stop. He just runs and runs with me. I feel like I'm going to fall off, but I never do. I always wake up first."

She made a restless splashing sound in the water, once again conjuring up an erotic picture for Dash.

Sounding hoarse to his own ears, he said, "Tell me what you're doing, Molly."

"I'm pouring shampoo into my hand."

He closed his eyes and pictured the thick, golden liquid puddling in her upturned palm. "What else?"

"Now I'm washing my hair."

Her arms would be lifted over her head, revealing those small, wonderful breasts. They would be slick with warm water, Dash guessed. She'd have her eyes closed and her head tilted back. Perhaps her mouth was parted.

He wished he could be in there with her. Holding her. Listening to her talk. He wanted to know more of her dreams. He wanted to know about *her* favorite teacher, her childhood hopes, the things that made her laugh. The things that turned her on.

Through the door, he said on a rasp, "Rub some shampoo on your breasts, Molly. Then tell me what it feels like."

"I don't think that's a good idea."

"Do it, please."

"But..."

"I just want to picture you doing it."

A moment later, she said only, "Umm..."

Dash grabbed the nearest towel bar with both hands and hung on for dear life.

She said, "Do you have a tub over there, Dash?"

"No," he managed to say from between gritted teeth. "Just a shower."

"Too bad. But— What's in the medicine cabinet?"

"What? Aspirin, I guess."

"Any oil?"

Clever girl. Exciting, bewitching, wonderful girl. Breathless, Dash ransacked the cupboards and found a bottle of baby oil someone had left there after sunbathing last summer. "Got it!"

She laughed, soft and low. "Good. Now pour some into your hand."

"Molly—"

"Do it. I want you to imagine my hands caressing your chest. The oil will be good for your skin, and I— I want to pretend I'm learning your body. I'll be your lover."

Dash gulped and fumbled with the lid on the bottle. In a moment, though, his hands were overflowing with smooth, warm oil. It spread easily and felt delicious between his fingers. Molly's voice mesmerized him, and he touched himself tentatively at first. She talked to him for a long time, her voice low and sensual from the other bathroom. It was easy to picture her lying in the fragrant water, bathing herself with closed eyes, an expression of ecstasy on her fine features as she spoke. He could imagine her slender hands exploring his body, memorizing each contour, enjoying every gasp her touch elicited.

His mouth felt incredibly dry. He longed to be kissing her, holding her, rubbing the slick oil into her golden skin. He wanted to penetrate her defenses with sensual caresses, to bring her to the brink of pleasure over and over. He wanted to be inside her, tight and velvety. He longed to feel her taut belly against his own, hear her breathe and match the pounding of her heartbeat with his.

"God, Molly, I can't stand it!"

"Yes, you can, Dash."

"I want to break down this door."

She laughed. "You'll ravish me and leave me sinking in this water."

"I'd never ravage you, Miss Molly. I want to break in there and carry you to my bed."

"And then?"

"I want to make loud, hard, hot love to you. And then," he said, "I think I want to talk. Afterward."

Her laughter was light, but breathless, too, as if she'd reached the limit of her self-control. She said, "I'm getting out of the tub now."

Dash leaned his forehead against the door and listened to the splash of water. He heard her fumble for a towel, then imagined her sleek body disappearing into a cloud of cotton. She dried her legs slowly, maybe even taking the two ends of the towel in hand to buff that beautifully round bottom of hers.

"Molly," he groaned. "I want you so badly."

"I've told you before. I'm not that kind of woman, Dash."

"This is it?" he demanded. "This is all I get?"

"Do you remember what you did to me this morning? Touching me?"

"I didn't excite you like this."

"Says who?" she challenged, laughing so musically that Dash wondered if she hadn't leaned against the door and felt his body heat through the wood. She said, "Take a shower now, Dash. Or you'll be late for dinner."

"You're a witch! How can I think of food now?"

"Are you frustrated?"

"Let me in, and I'll show you—"

"No, no, I've got to get dressed now. But thank you, Dash. I enjoyed this. You know, I think I like you."

He couldn't believe it. But she left. She abandoned him, leaving Dash to listen to the sound of water draining out of her bathtub and wondering what the hell she meant.

Growling like a frustrated boar, Dash stormed over to the shower. He yanked the lever, and water cascaded into the shower stall. Cold water. *Very* cold water.

At dinner Molly feared Dash might burn her to a cinder with his gaze. If it hadn't been for his children, she thought he probably would have thrown her down next to the succotash and made love to her in the middle of the table.

But his children were there, lined up like three little angels with dirty faces, exchanging sly glances when Dash finally appeared with wet hair and a thunderous expression on his brow.

"What's the matter with you, boyo?" Dillon demanded, noticing Dash's mood.

"Shut up," said Dash.

"Tell him, Pop!" Montgomery cheered.

"Behave yourself," Dash snapped at him, "or you'll be sent to your room."

Montgomery was a dark-eyed urchin with the same widow's peak Molly had noticed on his father. She had been gruffly introduced to him when she arrived in the dining room.

The room was large and lit by a two-tiered crystal chandelier. French doors opened onto the terrace. Underfoot lay an old, somewhat frayed oriental rug. The dishes and flatware, however, were ordinary and chipped from long use. The two older children had brought cans of soda to the table, and Dillon had two bottles of beer sitting at his place.

Montgomery turned eagerly to Molly. "I don't mind getting sent to my room. I have a race-car set."

Molly made a pretense of eating her salad, avoiding Dash's gaze and devoting her attention to the youngest child. "Oh, really? Do you like to race cars?"

"No, I mostly take them apart, see."

"Oh."

Montgomery popped a large black olive into his mouth and chewed it noisily, eyeing Molly with an expression of interest on his face. "Y'know," he said, very seriously, "you're a really pretty lady."

"Why, thank you."

"I have a friend who's got red hair, too. Her name's Jan."

"She's in your class at school?"

"Yep." He began putting black olives on the tips of his fingers. "Once, Jan pulled up her shirt and let me see her breasts."

Dash cleared his throat warningly.

But Montgomery didn't seem to hear. Still wedging olives into place and looking earnestly at Molly, he said, "I don't suppose you could—"

Dash intervened before the suggestion was out of Montgomery's mouth. "Young man, I think you'd better tell Patreen you'll have your dinner in your room."

Montgomery grinned. "Can I play with my race cars?"

"Whatever. Just stay out of trouble."

Montgomery obediently slid out of his chair, waving his black-tipped fingers at the family. Dash gave him a swat on the backside—more reassuring than punishing, Molly decided, and the boy gave a skip before bolting for freedom.

St. John was laughing. "Boy, Gummy's growing up, isn't he? Curious little brat, huh?"

"Eat your food, St. John."

"What's the matter, man?" the teenager taunted. "Did Gummy say something that hits a little too close to the bone? Like maybe *you* never got a chance to see somebody's—"

Dash gave his eldest son a single raised eyebrow. "This subject is closed before it gets started."

"Why?"

"Because it's not table conversation, that's why. Choose a more appropriate time and place."

"Other people talk about stuff like this," St. John objected. "Why, Mom says it's important to discuss sex openly—"

"Your mother isn't here at the moment."

"Yeah, right. She's the boss, huh?" St. John looked surly. "And you don't have any responsibilities where we're concerned. You wish we'd never happened!"

Dash set down his cutlery, and Molly held her breath, waiting for an explosion. But with remarkable control, Dash said, "All right. I'll admit I haven't been around enough for you. What exactly would you like to talk about, St. John?"

"Safe sex," the boy said promptly.

"By God," Dillon roared, "I won't have this kind of talk!"

Although the room sizzled with tension, Dash ignored his father and addressed his son. "St. John, I think you've brought up this subject just to start trouble, but if you're genuinely—"

"I thought safe sex was about *stopping* trouble. Or don't you know anything about it, man? You and the redhead making babies these days?"

Dash's hands tightened on the tablecloth. "You're on thin ice, young man."

The boy laughed and fished in the pocket of his shapeless shorts. An instant later, he came up with a foil packet, which he flipped insolently at his father. "Here, ever see one of these?"

Dash picked up the condom and turned it over in his fingers, glowering at the teenager. "Now I know you're trying to start trouble."

St. John shrugged. "I got a couple dozen, if you need 'em."

"I don't need them."

"Oho!" St. John chortled. "Too bad, man. You gotta use it or lose it, y'know."

Dash said nothing. Although Molly silently begged him to keep going, he couldn't do it.

He got up from the table and left the room.

St. John and Nikki stared after him, then broke into giggles. But Molly thought their laughter was forced and uneasy.

"What's going on?" Dillon demanded as Dash slammed the door. "What did he say?"

Molly threw her napkin down and ran after Dash. She caught up with him on the veranda outside the kitchen. He heard her footsteps and turned on her sharply, then relaxed when he realized who had followed him.

"Oh, it's you."

Molly planted herself directly in his path. "Dash, go back in there and finish what you started."

He shook his head and kept his voice low. "The kid's just trying to get a rise out of me."

Instinctively Molly took his hand in her own and squeezed. Like Dash, she spoke softly to avoid being overheard by someone in the house. "Of course he is! But St. John *needs* something. He just can't find a way to ask for it."

"He knows what he's doing."

"No, he doesn't. He's just pushing for a reaction—any reaction! It's up to you to go back in there and find out what he wants."

"Forget it."

"You can't run away."

"I'm not running away!"

"You're his father! You can't let him get away with being rude. And you can't deny that he's honestly looking for information from you. He's just doing it wrong."

Dash sent a glare in the direction of the dining room windows. "I ought to slap him."

"That's silly, and you know it. Go back and try something else."

But he shook his head. "I can't. I just can't say what's on my mind. I'll go too far and push him farther away."

"How can you be sure of that unless you try? You can't keep your emotions locked up like this. Too much self-control is a waste of energy."

"*You* say that? The Queen of Self-Control?"

She smiled ruefully. "Okay, I deserve that. But it's really true in your case, Dash. Don't miss out on fatherhood the way Dillon did."

"What?"

"Give a little," Molly urged. "Let him know you love him by *saying* so. Take a chance."

Dash pulled Molly into the shelter of a hemlock hedge. There the evening air was cool and shadowed. "I'd like to see *you* take a chance."

"Dash—"

"It goes both ways, doesn't it?"

Molly whispered. "Dash, I'm not ready to go to bed with you."

"I can make your body feel wonderful."

"Yes, you can. But sex alone isn't enough."

Exasperated, he said, "What do you want me to say?"

She laughed unsteadily. "I'm not looking for declarations of love. That's ridiculous, because I hardly know you. But we *are* strangers."

"When I held you today and touched you—"

"I know, I know. I nearly melted in your lap. But that's physical, and I want—I need—something more. We all need something more from you! Dash, do you know I've learned more about you from Mrs. O'Shay than I have from you?"

He frowned. "What did Patreen tell you?"

"Nothing. Maybe everything. I'm not sure. Look, I'm just not capable of having meaningless sex with anyone—even you."

Dash's hand came up and cupped her face, tipping it gently. "I guess I'll have to convince you."

But Molly stopped him before he could kiss her. Inside, she felt bitterly disappointed. He couldn't open up. He had to rely on the sexual chemistry. No wonder his marriage had been a failure.

Before she could stop herself, Molly asked, "Is this what happened with your wife?"

"What?"

"Were you so damned tight with her, too?" Molly tugged free from his grip. "You want the rest of us to be open and relaxed, but you can't handle being vulnerable yourself, can you?"

"I don't know what you're talking about."

"Of course you don't," Molly said harshly, turning away.

He grabbed her arm. "What does my ex-wife have to do with us?"

"It's not just her. It's everybody in your life. You won't let anyone get close."

"Oh, for God's sake—"

"Yes?" she prompted. "What do you want to say? Just let it out. Quit being so damned strong and let loose for once!"

"This is ridiculous."

"Dash—"

But she'd gone too far.

Dash spun on his heel and left her in the shadows.

Seven

Dash didn't sleep well. He thrashed with his pillow and grumbled to himself and finally gave up and reached to the nightstand to turn on a light. It nearly blinded him. With an oath, he blinked and fumbled for the clock. Four in the morning.

All he could think about was Molly and what he'd said to her.

What a jerk he'd been.

He sat up irritably and reached for the folder on the nightstand. He hoped an hour of studying the vet bills might put him back to sleep.

But he couldn't read the numbers for more than a minute without his mind wandering. He slammed the folder down and flopped back against his pillow to fume.

"That woman is driving me crazy," he muttered.

Did she have to be so beautiful? So quick to nail him when he was wrong? So blasted arousing all the time? So *right?*

"Okay, okay, I *should* have gone back to talk to St. John," Dash said to himself. "But what the hell was I supposed to say to him?"

It was an age-old problem for Dash. In his imagination, he saw it as a barrier, a huge stone wall that he had to climb to reach other people. But he couldn't get over it, and he couldn't break it down. He didn't have the ability to communicate with his son.

Or his father. Or his ex-wife. And now with Molly Pym.

From somewhere in the house, Dash suddenly heard a door close with a stealthy click.

"Who in the world is up at this hour?"

Dash slid out of bed and reached for his jeans. In another minute, he was out in the dim hallway, but no sound could be heard from there. Then he saw a thin strip of light underneath Molly's door.

Dash hesitated. He didn't want another confrontation. He'd made her angry earlier, and facing Molly was hard enough when she was calm. But a magnetic force somehow drew him to her door. He found himself trying the knob, and was surprised to find that it turned in his hand.

"Molly?" He kept his voice low. "Molly, you awake?"

He eased into her room. "Molly?"

She was gone. Dash knew it before he saw her empty bed. She'd left her light on, and her bed had been slept in but not made up again. Dash spun around, then breathed a sigh of relief when he saw her suitcase was lying open on the dresser. Her toothbrush and comb had been left in the bathroom, too.

"So she hasn't flown the coop," he murmured.

He sped quickly into the hallway and down the stairs, hoping to find her happily ensconced at the kitchen table with a bowl of cereal or a midnight snack. With a pang of guilt, Dash remembered he'd ruined her dinner the night before. But Molly wasn't in the kitchen.

Where in hell had she gone?

Molly let herself out the French doors and tiptoed past Dash's open bedroom window in her sock feet. She thought she was perfectly quiet, but suddenly she heard him mutter a curse and sit up in bed. An instant later, his light stabbed on, and Molly leapt into the safety of a shadow.

Holding her breath in the cool night air, she heard him talking to himself, then a rattle of paper. She eased along the veranda, heading for a set of outside steps she'd scouted the evening before. A simple latched gate stood at the top of the stairs, and she quietly pulled it open and let herself through. It made a tiny click when it closed again—hardly loud enough to be heard inside the house—but Molly decided not to wait around, just in case. She hustled down the steps, circled the back of the silent house by way of the terrace and let herself into the unlocked front door to get her boots on.

Finally ready, she slipped out of the house again and headed across the lawn in the darkness. Her hands were full of the tools she'd need before dawn.

The night was still and cool, the air slightly damp with mist. It felt good to breathe, and the swish of grass beneath her boots made a queerly restless sound.

From the opposite hillside, she heard the whistling whicker of a horse.

"I'm coming," she whispered.

Mashed Potato stood like a statue in the middle of his shadowy meadow. The moonlight seemed to pour down from the sky and set his coat alight. His head was tilted high as he watched her progress up the hill. His ears were stiff, his eyes flashing liquid.

Molly approached him slowly, and softly sang an old song she'd learned from her father. The words were ancient Celtic, and she didn't know what they said exactly. But the meaning was clear—to her and to the colt. It was a love song.

From under the fence came Seabiscuit. The old dog wagged his tail and limped toward Molly, happy to see her.

"Hiya, Biscuit." She knelt and cradled his head affectionately. "You're doing your job, aren't you? How's it going?"

Biscuit licked her face and whuffed in his throat, but he seemed to understand the need to be quiet. He turned and led the way to Mashed Potato.

Molly crawled through the fence, then stood up cautiously to face the colt across the dark grass.

He watched her intently, but the muscles beneath his shining coat didn't twitch with anxiety. The sound of Molly's low voice intrigued him, and he studied her for a long moment. When she pulled a mint leaf from her pocket, he lifted his head higher and smelled the wind. The scent that reached his nostrils seemed to interest him, so he paced forward quickly, neck out-stretched.

But twelve feet away, he stopped dead, suddenly wary again.

Molly spoke more of the language she'd learned long ago, making her voice musical and letting the tune carry her own spirit. She held the sprig of mint out to Mashed Potato, allowing the scent to tease him closer.

And he came. Slowly, but without fear. A few steps away, he halted again and stared deeply into Molly's face, looking suddenly wise and magical. With wings, he'd have been Pegasus. Despite his youth, a certain noble aura surrounded him. His blue blood was apparent in the princely curve of his neck, the superb length of bone and tautness of muscle. His eyes didn't roll white, but remained fixed and curious.

He nibbled the leaf, as if judging the flavor, then tugged it completely from Molly's grasp. She let him have it and remained very still while he chewed and swallowed the offering. For a full minute, Molly held still and murmured love words. He stepped closer and sniffed her hands, inhaling the mint and imprinting the scent in his mind.

Carefully, Molly touched him. She felt the smooth steel of his muscles and the electric current of his nerves. She felt his heart beating and his mind ticking rapidly as he listened to her words. Once, he swung his head around, but he didn't bite. He nuzzled her curiously and tugged her shirt in his teeth.

"Another piece, you greedy boy?" She had a second sprig of mint in her pocket and teased him with it before letting the colt steal it. He savored the flavor.

It didn't take long once he trusted her. Perhaps an hour at the most. The horizon began to lighten, then turned pink, and the first sounds of birds started to echo in the nearby trees. By the time the sun peeked over the hillside, Mashed Potato was as docile as a child's pony.

He played with Molly's hair and snuffled at her clothes. He allowed her to smooth her hands along his sides, and nudged her when she stopped scratching the spot behind his ear. Before long, he was happy to wear the rope halter she'd brought. The rough game appealed to him, too. He followed her around in circles, spun on his haunches to head her off as she dashed this way and that. Gently he bumped her with his nose and stamped his forefoot in the grass.

But suddenly he threw up his head and snorted.

Molly turned to look in the cool light of sunrise, and saw the figure of a man leaning ghostlike against the fence.

"Dash," she breathed, feeling absurdly guilty.

No use pretending he wasn't there. Although the lesson wasn't over, Molly left the colt and walked slowly across the meadow to the man who stood eerily still, as if he'd been sleepwalking.

His first words were "I wanted to believe you could do this. But I wasn't completely sure."

"You're staring at me like I just grew long ears and a tail."

Dash shook his head, bewildered. "I—I don't understand. What is it about you? You haven't done anything different. It's just—well, it's like magic."

She laughed and leaned her arms on the fence, propping her chin on her folded hands. "Maybe it *is* magic."

"I don't understand."

Molly shrugged. "I'm doing what you're paying me to do."

"But—but—he was wild yesterday." Dash's gaze traveled past Molly and fixed on the colt. "He was another animal. My God, you were *playing* with him just now. It's a wonder he didn't kill you."

She said, "He's not the only thing that needs taming around here."

Dash met her eyes then. Still behaving like a man in a dream, he stepped to the fence and touched her face. There were calluses on his hands, but he seemed to be seeking some message on her face. "You're a puzzle, Molly Pym."

"I think I'm very simple. It's you who's hard to understand."

He dropped his hand away, pain flicking across his expression. "Last night—I was an idiot, I know. I'm sorry for all of it."

"You've got some things to learn about parenting," she said gently.

His answering smile came slowly. "I'm all wrong for it."

"You can change. You have to learn to share."

He shook his head. "I've been on my own too long."

Though she hung on to her smile, Molly felt her heart swell as she thought of the little boy whose mother died when he was young, whose father was a bullying blowhard known for loving only winners. She thought of the young man who married an accomplished young woman of privilege and couldn't bring himself to share her life.

"You could try."

"It's a waste of time."

"Not for you. Dash, you've done so much in your life. Mountains, oceans—you've triumphed over them all. This isn't nearly as hard."

"For me, it is."

"They're only children, Dash."

"They're not the whole problem."

Molly's concern grew as she realized there was more troubling Dash than three troublesome children. It seemed he harbored more secrets.

He glanced around them at the hills, the green fields and the distant house, now just touched by the new sunlight. Uncertainly he said, "I want to keep this farm, Molly. It never meant much to me when I was younger, but now it's important. Thing is, we're in trouble."

"What kind of trouble?"

"Money. My father's made a mess of things, and I— Oh, hell, I'm not sure I can fix it. It's too hard to keep everything in balance. I don't handle people very well—"

"You've handled me from the start," she said dryly.

He smiled. "Not as much as I wanted to. But the rest—the bankers and my father, now my own children—they're all cogs in an engine that I've got to keep oiled somehow—at least until we have a steady income."

Molly started to understand the whole picture. "That's Mashed Potato's job, isn't it? To provide a steady income."

He met her gaze. "I can't tell you how badly we need him, Molly."

Despite the fence between them, she reached for Dash's hand and clasped it in her two. "Don't worry. He'll be ready soon."

"How?"

"I can do it. He's wonderful, really. He just needs to trust, and then he'll do what comes naturally. You can trust me."

"You're amazing," Dash said softly. "In a lot of ways."

She saw the heat in his eyes and said on a laugh, "Don't start, O'Donnelly—"

"I'm not talking about the physical stuff. I—well," he finished awkwardly, "I'm glad you're here, Molly."

That was a start, Molly thought. She couldn't expect him to say more. "All right," she said briskly and with humor, "that's enough mutual admiration for one day. Go away and leave us alone. I'll spend the morning with your precious colt."

"I'd like to stay," Dash said, still holding her hand, "but I've got a meeting."

"See you later."

Molly couldn't help herself. Impulsively she leaned over the fence and kissed him on the cheek. Dash's hand came up to cup her head and make her lips linger. But he didn't move to kiss her back. Instead, Molly thought she felt a quiver in his hand.

Dash wasn't sure what was happening, exactly. He only knew that he spent the next few days working in his office and hungering for the sight of Molly passing by his window.

She was amazing. On that first day, she played with Mashed Potato and gained his confidence. By the end of the second day, she had a bridle on him and used a lunge line. In four days, she was on his back. And all the while, Dash had the feeling she was teaching *him,* not just his horse.

She moved Mashed Potato to a small paddock beside the stallion barn, a place, she claimed, where the colt felt comfortable. A place where she could keep an eye on Dash, too. She also fed him hot mashes and plenty of vitamins—the colt, not Dash. Mashed Potato began to gain weight and look less like a starving animal. Dash, on the other hand, wanted no food and even quit smoking cigars. They always ended up looking as if they'd been gnawed by a frustrated squirrel.

Through patience, stubborn and obvious love, Molly trained the colt. By the end of the week, Molly was riding Mashed Potato on the track and introducing him to the stable staff, one by one. It was not an uncommon sight to see one of the grooms warily standing his ground while the once-ornery colt sniffed him over. At last, Molly found someone who was comfortable enough with Mashed Potato to become his regular care-giver. A young girl, Alice Greenspan, happily took the job—a promotion from her position as a lowly hot walker.

Molly also managed to make friends with everybody at O'Donnelly Farms. Dash caught her having morning tea with his secretary and making a salad in the kitchen one evening with Patreen O'Shay.

The next day Patreen announced she needed to pay a visit to her sister in New Jersey.

"Now?" Dash cried, dismayed. "You want to leave while my kids are here?"

"I'm catching the train in the morning," Patreen said, slapping Dash's hand as he reached to snitch a predinner roll from a basket on the counter. "You can take care of those children yourself."

"Are you kidding? Patreen, I have the deepest respect for your sister, but—" Dash caught the glance Patreen exchanged with Molly, who was perched on a kitchen stool and trying to look innocent while chopping vegetables with a large knife. "Wait a minute," he said. "Do you have something to do with this situation, Miss Molly?"

"Me? I don't even know Patreen's sister."

Dash glowered at the two conniving females. "Isn't it a funny coincidence that Patreen's sister needs her just several days after you decide I need to participate more in the everyday activities of those kids?"

"A funny coincidence, all right. What are you going to feed the kids for breakfast?"

"Can't they feed themselves?"

Patreen snorted, and Molly laughed. "Dash, they may act like sophisticated monsters, but they really need your help. I'd suggest cereal and toast, just to keep things simple. And juice. What about lunch?"

"The nearest McDonald's?"

Molly and Patreen looked at each other. "It's a start," they said in unison.

Taking care of his children for three days wasn't as bad as Dash feared. Montgomery was the only one who needed nearly constant supervision, and he turned out to be an entertaining kid.

"C'mon, Dad," he begged. "Let me drive the Jag again, huh? Will you?"

"I never should have let you do it the first time."

But holding Montgomery on his lap and helping the boy guide the long-nosed car slowly along the farm lanes had been the highlight of an otherwise unpleasant day.

The bankers turned up—six men in suits with bulging briefcases, who announced it was time Dash considered consolidating some of his loans and selling off a few assets to fortify his financial position.

"There's nothing to sell," he told them. "No equipment, no land—"

"How about some yearlings?" suggested old Jim Wilkins, a longtime Saratoga banker who knew the racing business almost as well as the families who owned farms in the area. "Are you sending any stock to the sale at Dansford next month?"

Dash had hoped to hang on to all but two yearlings, but he knew he'd have to part with more of them in order to raise much-needed cash.

Backed into a corner, he agreed to sell at least a dozen promising youngsters. When the bankers departed, Dash sought out his father in one of the barns to break the news.

Dillon was surprisingly philosophical, though regretful about parting with some of his favorites. "We'll go through the list tomorrow," he told Dash. "I knew we'd have to thin out the crop eventually."

"I'm sorry, Pop."

Dillon didn't meet his son's eye as he said gruffly, "Well, at least we've got Mashed Potato."

Dash grinned. "What changed your tune? I thought you were ready to send that colt to the nearest glue factory."

Strolling out into the afternoon sunlight, Dillon gazed pensively across the lane to an exercise field where Molly Pym could be seen schooling Mashed

Potato. Dillon said, "That girl's done all right with him."

"She's a damned miracle worker, and you know it."

Dillon must have heard something in Dash's tone, because he looked sharply at his son. "She's not bad," he said. "But she's no trainer of racehorses."

"What do you mean? Take a look at the way she's got him behaving—"

"That's just it," Dillon snapped, pointing as Molly stood in the stirrups to execute figure eights. "She's going to turn him into a saddle horse fit for the local 4-H Club! We need a colt with fire in him."

Dash knew his father was right. But he'd been so caught up in watching Molly's progress that he'd lost sight of his goal. "What do you suggest?"

Dillon kept his steely gaze trained on the colt as he pirouetted on Molly's command and set off lickety-split along the fence rail. "I think it's time she turned over Mashed Potato to me."

"But, Pop..."

"You have a problem, boyo?"

Dash was torn. "She's developed a relationship with that colt. It's—well, they're friends, in a way—"

"What nonsense!" Dillon exploded. "It's time to break them up before he's only good for giving pony rides at the county fair! I want him on the track under a jockey by next week. Willy Bartman is coming up soon. Maybe he'd like a crack at Mashed Potato."

Dash could understand the wisdom of his father's words.

But he hated to take Mashed Potato out of Molly's care. Not yet. It seemed like a rotten trick.

"What's the matter, boyo? You getting soft on me?"

"No," Dash said defensively. But he couldn't help picturing Molly's face when she got the news.

"You can't be tenderhearted in this business," Dillon advised. "Not over a horse."

"I know."

"And not over a girl, either. Not if she jeopardizes the future of a good colt like that."

Dash found himself gritting his teeth. "All right," he said at last. "But I want to be the one to break the news to her. Got that? I don't want you getting into a fight with her over this."

"Got it," Dillon said amiably. "You'll tell her tonight?"

Dash withheld a sigh. "Yes."

He hated the idea of tearing Molly and Mashed Potato apart—especially since they were getting to be such a delightful sight around the farm.

Besides, if her job was finished, Molly would have no reason to stay at O'Donnelly Farms anymore.

Eight

"Oh, thank heavens you're back," Molly cried, catching sight of Dash as he came through the kitchen door later that evening. Her red hair was tied up on top of her head, but the steamy heat had freed some curls. "Quick," she said, "stop standing there doing nothing and make some hamburgers. Montgomery is starving."

Dash picked up a package of ground beef left on the kitchen counter. "What am I supposed to do with this? And where is Montgomery?"

"He's upstairs getting his clothes changed, and Nikki's setting the picnic table so we won't be late for the hayride."

Dash was sure he'd heard wrong. "The what?"

Molly bounded around the kitchen counter, looking vital and happy. She had a spatula in one hand and a half-frosted chocolate cupcake in the other. "Julio has organized a hayride for tonight. Isn't it great? In honor of your father's birthday.''

That surprised him. "It's Pop's birthday?"

Molly's blue eyes opened wide. "You don't know your own father's birthday?"

"Why should I? Why should *you?*" he demanded. "I thought you hated his guts."

"I do," Molly said cheerily. "But I love hayrides, and Julio says tonight's going to be perfect. Isn't Julio a treasure?"

"Yeah, a treasure, all right."

"He's even got a bonfire ready for us. All we have to do is light a match when we get back. St. John just took his bike over to the Quik Shopper to get some marshmallows."

Dash marveled at the idea of his eldest son willingly doing anything remotely helpful. "How did you convince him to do that?"

"It was his suggestion. He's really not such a bad kid, Dash. You've done wonders with him this week."

Dash knew his son hadn't responded to anything *he'd* done during the week. Any change in St. John's behavior was entirely due to Molly's ceaseless good cheer and determination.

As she passed by on her way to the refrigerator, Dash snagged Molly by the arm, and her momentum spun her around and neatly into his embrace. Dash immediately gathered her up, though he'd been fighting that urge for days. "Miss Molly," he said, "you've turned out to be something really special this week."

She didn't seem to mind his arms around her. In fact, she relaxed in Dash's embrace and held up the spatula. "You haven't done so badly yourself, O'Donnelly."

He gave the spatula an experimental lick. "You may not say that when I tell you what I've come here to—"

But Dash stopped himself. Molly's upturned face was too beautiful to spoil with bad news. Besides, a tantalizing drop of chocolate frosting had somehow managed to find its way to her cheek. Dash used one forefinger to wipe it away, then licked the sweetness off his finger. It melted on his tongue, but he felt like melting into her arms.

Molly grinned, her eyes lazy lidded as she watched him lick the frosting. "Taste good?"

"I can think of something even better."

Her smile didn't waver. "I thought you'd lost interest."

"In you? No, I haven't lost interest."

He'd fought his need for her all week, and it was like battling a dozen sumo wrestlers with high-octane testosterone seething in their veins. Every day, he swore he'd keep his distance. Every night, he thanked heaven he'd managed to keep his hands off her.

"It's been a struggle," he admitted cautiously.

"Why did you do it?"

"I'm not sure," he said honestly. "It just seemed like a better strategy."

"Is it working?"

"Let's see," Dash murmured, stealing closer to press a tiny kiss on her delicious mouth.

It was a mistake to think he could give her one kiss and be satisfied. Molly dropped the spatula and slid her hand up his chest. She looped one arm around his neck, drawing Dash's mouth deeply against her own. She tasted sweet and warm, and the dizzy wave that threatened to overwhelm Dash swept up at once, clouding his wits, drowning his senses. Her lips parted, and her tongue met his with teasing purpose. She even laughed a little, and curled the ends of his hair in her fingertips.

I'm lost, Dash thought.

"Stop," he begged, when he managed to break the kiss With firm hands, he pushed her back, then changed his mind and lifted Molly off her feet and sat her abruptly on the counter. His breath felt tight in his chest. "Stop, before I take your clothes off here and now. God, Molly, how I want you."

She set down her cupcake and wound both arms around his neck. She wrapped her long legs around his hips. She used them to pull him closer, and they bumped their foreheads together. "It's different now, though, isn't it?"

Dash subjected himself to the gentle caress of her fingers on the back of his neck. "I keep thinking if I do something wrong, I'll screw up everything."

"You can't do anything wrong."

Closing his eyes, he said, "I don't want to lose you."

Molly didn't answer. The words seemed to change things. After a long moment, she began to kiss his face, all over, with tiny, gentle kisses that—he supposed—were intended to soothe the savage beast, but actually inflamed Dash to the point of groaning. Molly's legs hugged him, and he felt as if his jeans were going to burst. She was so sexy—smelling of outdoors and sweet kitchen scents. Dash forced himself to plant his palms on the counter on either side of her hips. He tried to control himself, but suddenly his brain was full of erotic images.

Breathing gently in his ear, she said, "I think of you at night."

He groaned again. "Don't tell me."

"I do. I wonder what we'd be like together."

Her nibbles progressed to his neck, and Dash suppressed a shudder of longing. "Molly, I—I should warn you. I'm not a gentleman in bed."

"No?"

"And you make me crazier than anyone I've ever known."

Her teeth were sharp on his earlobe. "Were you crazy with your ex-wife?"

"That was different."

"How?"

"She was— All we ever did was go to bed. There wasn't anything else."

"What was good, though? The sex?"

"Terrific." He couldn't help himself, and began to massage the delectable curve of Molly's bottom. "But look what happened."

"Your kids are great, Dash."

"But the marriage was a mess. From the start, it was terrible, and it went downhill from there. It was all wrong. I don't want to go through it again. Not with you."

She pulled back and eyed him thoughtfully. "So you held back with me this week, didn't you?"

"Yes, to prevent a disaster," Dash said at length. "I want you in my life, Molly."

She was silent for a long time, stroking Dash's cheek with her thumb and studying his eyes.

Though the words seemed to burn in his throat, Dash said, "I don't want to sacrifice what we could have for sex."

She smiled a little and slid her fingertips down his chest. "Even great sex?"

He laughed, sounding strangled even to his own ears as her caress reached his belt and lingered there. "It could be really great, couldn't it?"

She wiggled her eyebrows. "Especially if you're no gentleman."

"But is it a mistake?"

"If it feels good, what could go wrong?" Her expression was both lascivious and pleased. She looked happy, Dash realized. They had reached a new plane, though he didn't understand exactly how it had happened. All he understood was her willingness.

If she slid her hand lower and touched him just then, Dash was sure he'd explode.

But fortunately, they heard the scrape of sneakered feet on the terrace, and they sprang apart before Nikki made her entrance into the kitchen.

"Whew!" she cried. "It's hot out there! Daddy, will you open the umbrella on the table?"

At that moment, Dash wasn't sure which made him happier—hearing Nikki call him Daddy or sensing Molly wanted him in her bed that night. But a glance at Molly's secret smile made up his mind.

As soon as the damn hayride was over, he planned to climb between her sheets and make her shriek with ecstasy.

A hayride, Molly decided, was one of the most erotic experiences known to man.

It wasn't the mess of dusty, sneezy hay, the bone-shattering jounce of the wagon, or the corny songs sung by deliriously goofy children, for those particular elements were not especially pleasant, if the truth be known. Nor was Molly particularly happy to spend the evening listening to Dillon O'Donnelly bellowing melodramatic Irish ballads in an excruciatingly bad baritone.

But lying in Dash's arms and plucking bits of hay out of his shirt and feeling his heart beating just beneath her shoulder blade made her absurdly excited.

It all started when she watched Dash effortlessly boost all his kids up onto the wagon, then vault up himself as easily as you please. Now and then she forgot he was a world-class athlete, but when he extended his hand down to her, eyes sparkling in the growing twilight, Molly grabbed his hand and felt herself hauled up beside him as lightly as if she'd been a leaf.

It was a hot night. The sun had gone down, but had left the air steamy with humidity. Sitting in a heap of hay should have been hellishly uncomfortable. But Dash kicked a pile of hay into a nest and made no secret of pulling Molly into his lap when it was ready. He wrapped one long arm around her body to keep her there. The other hand he used to hold fast to the waistband of Montgomery's shorts to keep the boy from falling off the wagon.

Nikki glanced at the picture of her father holding Molly and said disdainfully, "Aren't you a little *old* for that, Dad?"

"You've got a lot to learn, young lady," he shot back cheerfully.

"It's gross," said St. John.

Dash craned a look around at him. "What's the matter with you?"

Molly had also noticed St. John's coolness that evening, but she kept quiet, hoping that Dash would

make the first move to open a dialogue with the teenager.

St. John shrugged. "Nothing."

"That face doesn't look like nothing."

"I was just thinking of mom, that's all."

"Your mother?" Dash repeated.

"Yeah, you know, the lady you have three kids
with. Or are you going to have more kids with Molly,
too?"

Molly herself said, "Does it bother you to see your
father with another woman?"

"No."

She poked Dash in the ribs to encourage him to talk.
He took a deep breath and said to St. John, "I don't
understand. Are you hoping I'll get back with your
mother?"

"No." But St. John didn't sound convincing.

"We've been divorced for five years. Surely she sees
other men."

St. John shook off the argument with a sulky shrug.
"She has dates once in a while. But nothing like this."
He indicated Molly with a jut of his chin.

"Like what?" Dash pressed.

"Well, she doesn't have her hands all over anybody."

"I'll bet she does," Dash said, "when you're not
looking."

St. John sat up angrily. "Don't talk about her like
that! You have no right to act like she's doing anything wrong when you're—you're—"

"St. John, my marriage to your mother is over. She
and I understood that a long time ago. I'm comfortable that she's making her own decisions these days."

Still angry, but with a lower voice, St. John said, "You didn't try to stay together."

"Maybe not hard enough," Dash agreed. "I loved her, and she loved me—I think we still do, but it wasn't the right kind of love for a marriage. We just can't live together."

"Because of us."

With heat, Dash objected. "That's ridiculous. The best part of our marriage was you kids. Believe me, we were delighted to have you."

"But?"

"But sometimes children aren't enough to keep two very different people together. It's not your fault. It's ours—mine and your mom's. Believe me, we'd all be in worse shape if we were still trying to live under the same roof."

Nikki said softly, "Did you really love her?"

Dash sighed and looked at Molly. She tried to give him a smile of encouragement. Reluctantly Dash turned to his children and said, "Yes, I loved her. I still do, in a way. But I knew I'd ruin her life if I forced my circumstances on her, and she— Well, your mother tried to change me, too, but soon figured out it was impossible. All the effort just made us more miserable."

"So you gave up on us."

"It must look that way," Dash said with a frown. "I never meant to give you that idea, but— Look, sometimes I wish I had never married your mom. We made some mistakes and hurt each other badly. But we also had some good stuff going, too. Your mother's a terrific woman. Smart and beautiful and—well, she taught me a lot about life."

Dash hesitated, then added, "To tell the truth, though, I'm learning even more from you three."

Montgomery frowned. "But you're a grown-up."

Dash laughed uneasily. "That doesn't mean I know everything. In the time you've been here, I've learned a lot of things—about myself as well as about you."

"Like what?"

"Well, like I wish I wasn't such a grouch all the time. You're actually kind of fun to have around."

Montgomery smiled. "Do you wish you had us more often?"

"Yes," Dash said. "I honestly do."

Looking mistrustful, Nikki said, "We've been pretty rotten, though."

Dash shrugged. "I was no angel when I was your age."

Dillon gave a laugh. "That's the truth!"

St. John looked curiously at his grandfather. "What was my dad like?"

With a devilish gleam in his eye, Dillon leaned forward. "Oh, a troublemaker from the very start. Did I ever tell you about the pony he tried to keep in his bedroom? Taught that nasty beast to climb steps, but couldn't get him down again until the whole second floor smelled like a stable! And he ran away from home when he was younger than you, by God—"

Hastily Dash said, "Let's not give these kids any more ideas, okay Pop?"

"Okay, boyo," Dillon agreed, leaning back in the hay once more with an amused air. "Let's just say he always knew his own mind and went off half-cocked most of the time, but he came around in the end. You're doing all right, son. And this little girl—" he pointed at Molly "—isn't such a bad choice as I thought."

Tartly, Molly said, "Thanks."

"Don't get me wrong," Dillon began.

"Oh, pipe down, old man."

He laughed.

St. John said suddenly, "I think you're okay, too, Miss Molly."

Surprised, Molly could say only, "Thanks."

St. John said, "I won't promise anything, but maybe Nikki's right. We've been kind of—well, you know."

The boy was on the brink of accepting her, Molly knew, and she tried to make it easier for him. "I know."

"If you're going to be around—I guess we better be nice to you."

"Only if you feel like it," Molly said.

"I feel like it," Montgomery said eagerly. "I like you, Molly. I think my mom would like you, too."

St. John said, "But she wouldn't like it if you tried to take her place."

"I won't do that," Molly said. "I'd rather be your friend."

Before the conversation could go any further, Dillon interrupted. "Let's sing something. Montgomery, have you ever heard 'The Shy Lass from Killikarney'?"

"No, Grampa." Young Montgomery seemed the only one immune to Dillon's terrible singing voice. "Teach it to me."

"My dear departed mother used to sing it when she thought I wasn't listening. Did I ever tell you about your Granny O'Donnelly, boyo?"

"Nope."

"Well, here's her favorite song."

He sang bawdy lyrics. The children giggled. Julio drove the horses. And Molly lay quietly between Dash's thighs and listened. At that moment, she felt absurdly proud of Dash. He hadn't gotten mad and stormed away, turning his back on the problem to avoid confronting it. For the first time, he'd allowed St. John to state his case and countered with his own honest feelings. He'd done well. She longed to lean her head against his chest and tell him so, but she didn't dare provoke St. John with anything resembling a further public display of affection.

So Molly contented herself with slipping one hand under the hay and finding Dash's there. They laced fingers in secret, and Dash squeezed. No promises made, but something had changed, all right.

Molly tipped a smile up at him, her heart brimming over. Until that evening, she'd felt the unmistakable urgency of sex that radiated constantly from Dash. But tonight that passion seemed combined with deeper emotions. Now, something more existed between them. Something good.

Oh, but it was hot! The heat seemed to beat down from the heavens. Ordinarily Molly would have longed to jump down and throw herself into the nearest pond to cool off, but somehow the heat was more erotic than annoying. She felt as if her flesh were melting. A wonderful lassitude crept over her, dulling her wits, but sharpening her other senses. She felt almost drugged.

All she could think about was Dash's powerful body beneath her own. His chest was broad and powerfully toned. The tight muscles of his belly bespoke years of hard exercise. It was impossible not to imagine how his long, supple legs might look without their casing of blue jeans.

Molly could also feel the suggestion of his arousal as she lay languidly against him, one hip riding comfortably against the slightly out-turned length of his right leg. As Dash laughed and spoke to his family, he allowed the fingers of one hand to absently trace designs on Molly's arm—designs that seemed to spell secret words meant only for her.

Before an hour had passed, she knew she was flushed from the heat—and the passion that was slowly building to an explosive climax. A flicker of heat lightning lit up the night sky overhead.

Dash found himself enjoying the evening. He hadn't expected to. But listening to his children loosen up and chatter like monkeys, he began to have a true sense of what he had missed as a parent. It made him sad at first.

But it was hard not to appreciate the second chance that lay before him. He'd been given another opportunity to be a father to his kids.

And all because of Molly.

Dash felt her lean body meld against his own frame, and he enjoyed the softness of her hip, the pleasant hint of her breast he saw as he peeped down the partially unbuttoned front of her shirt. The barest sheen of perspiration glowed on her skin there. If he'd been alone with her, Dash supposed he'd unfasten all those buttons and open the shirt completely. He imagined kissing her nipples one after the other, and rolling them on his tongue in the heat. He wanted to bury his face against her belly and tug her breeches from her

hips. Later, he'd tease her unmercifully with his mouth
until she wept with pleasure.

But the proximity of Nikki, Montgomery and the
ever-changing St. John prevented Dash from even
fondling Molly a little bit. He had to be content with
cradling her in his arms and hoping he wasn't going to
be embarrassed by the one part of his body he couldn't
control.

Julio drove along the lanes of O'Donnelly Farms
while Dillon led the children in assorted raucous Irish
songs and told them stories about their colorful family. At last, however, they reached the house, where a
bonfire had been laid. Julio wished them all good-
night and drove off toward the stables.

The backyard fire burned brightly and sent a stream
of sparks into the sky along with the piquant scent of
wood smoke. St. John had already cut marshmallow
sticks, and he showed his younger brother how to burn
the sticky treats into blackened masses of sugar. Nikki
was more careful, making sure hers were evenly
toasted all over before popping them into her mouth.
Dillon watched indulgently, drinking coffee from a
thermos.

Molly roasted one for Dash and made him eat it
from her fingers. In the light of the flames, her gaze
was full of a different kind of firelight.

At last, the kids tired of marshmallows and began
to complain of the heat. Molly suggested they go for
a swim, and Montgomery excitedly pulled off all his
clothes and dived naked into the pool to cool off.
Nikki and St. John, more adult, followed in their T-
shirts and shorts.

Dash was a little disappointed that Molly didn't follow suit. He'd have enjoyed seeing her clothes clinging to her delectable body.

It seemed forever, but finally Dillon marched off to bed, and the kids weren't far behind him.

"I'm gonna watch TV in my room," St. John declared, but he looked sleepy, and Dash doubted he'd last long.

"Now," Molly said to him when they were alone by the pool and she'd knelt before the Adirondack chair where he'd sprawled to watch the action. "What do you say we go for a swim ourselves?"

He was glad to have her to himself at last and wanted to enjoy the moment. "Now?"

"You have a better idea?"

Dash felt his heart slam into high gear. He reached for her arm and pulled Molly to kneel between his knees. Her curly red hair had frizzed into a bright halo, emphasizing her full mouth and Irish eyes. She leaned her elbows on his thighs as if staking a claim. He liked the feeling. Voice turning husky, Dash said, "I've had a lot of ideas since the day I met you, Miss Molly."

Her answering smile was wicked. "Such as?"

"I intended to kidnap you."

She widened her eyes, pretending fear. "And do what?"

"My feelings have changed on that subject," he admitted, relishing the supple delicacy of her body between his legs. "Now I want to keep you a prisoner. I want you all for myself. In my house and in my bed."

"Would you consider a long soak in a tub first?"

He liked the confidence in her grin and felt his insides stir. "With bubble bath?"

"As much as you like."

Dash's face must have reflected a lot of emotions, for she laughed and grabbed his hand. Molly pulled Dash to his feet. "What's the matter? Don't you believe me?"

"I just want to be sure you're ready."

"Oh, I'm ready," she said huskily. "More than ready."

She ran then, dragging Dash along in her wake. But once in the house, he overtook her easily, and swept Molly into his arms. She laughed, and the sound was better than any music he'd ever heard. Carrying her, he leapt up the staircase, down the private hallway and threaded his way into her room.

"Are you kidnapping me?" she asked, laughter in her eyes and her hands locked behind his neck.

"Yes."

"Oh, good." She nibbled his ear and whispered, "Do your worst."

In the back of his mind, he knew there was something he was supposed to tell her. But just then, Dash's brain was seething with something much more immediate. At last, she was in his power. She was ready and willing.

They were inside her room then. With a kick, Dash closed the door.

"Now then," he growled. "Let's get started."

Nine

Molly backed up until she felt her knees collide with the bed. "What are you going to do?"

"Watch you take off your clothes, for starters."

With a flick of his finger, Dash flipped on the lamp, bathing the room in a golden glow. He looked anything but golden, however. The half-light accentuated the way his jeans clung to his hips and the dark, scowling expression of his brow. "Be a good prisoner, Molly. Obey me, or I'll have to be more forceful."

"You wouldn't."

By way of answer, Dash reached behind himself and turned the lock on the closed door. Then he leaned against it, arms folded across his chest and a smile on his mouth. But there was a very serious glitter showing in his eye, too. "Of course I would. Now, start undressing, please."

"Are you trying to make me nervous?"

"I doubt that's possible."

The flutter in Molly's heart wasn't a result of nerves just then. It was the thrill of anticipation. With unsteady fingers, she began to unbutton her shirt. "Are you going to watch me like that all night?"

"Yes. Shirt first, please."

Her shirt fluttered to the bed. Molly always wore a T-shirt or tank top underneath, but tonight the wisp of her abbreviated top seemed inadequate. She hesitated, for underneath it she was naked.

"Take it off," Dash commanded.

"No choice, hmm?"

"None."

Molly obeyed, removing the tank top slowly, and instinctively clasping her arms to her breasts once it was off.

Dash shook his head. "I want to see you."

She feared his gaze might actually burn her skin, but when Molly dropped her arms, she wasn't in pain. She saw a shudder of longing cross Dash's face, and felt a flare of passion arrow down into her belly. It was exciting to be the sole object of a man's desire. The realization gave Molly more confidence.

"Now the boots," Dash said, decidedly hoarse.

Molly sat on the edge of the bed, bare breasted, and leaned back on her hands. She extended one booted foot toward him. "Help me."

He pushed away from the door and approached her, not taking his dark eyes from Molly's. He grabbed her boot, toe and heel, and drew it off slowly. He dropped it on the floor and did the same with the second one.

Then, as if unable to hold himself back any longer, he went down on one knee and reached to unfasten her breeches.

She said, "I thought I was supposed to do that."

His fleeting grin flashed. "You're too slow."

"Take your time, O'Donnelly. Or it might not last long."

He said, "It's going to last all night, Miss Molly."

Drawing off her breeches and panties in one fluid motion, Dash stripped her bare and let out a slow, pent-up breath when her long body was finally revealed to him. He ran one palm up her thigh and found the hot skin of her loins. He leaned close and kissed her just above the fine down between her legs. Molly's heart pounded so hard that she felt dizzy.

"Now you," she managed to say with a trembling voice.

She unfastened the buttons of his shirt herself, while Dash unbuckled his belt. His chest was beautifully muscled and covered in a crisp T-shaped growth of hair. She plunged her fingers into it and found herself leaning close to kiss him there—three, four, five times before licking the salty taste of his flat male nipples. Dash's breath caught in his throat.

In another second, she had somehow flattened him on the floor and they were wrestling with his boots and jeans. The rest of his physique was powerful and lightly tanned. Molly straddled him, and found his body sleek, sensitive and very hard. His skin felt hot under her fingers.

Dash ran his hands down her sides, cupped her bottom and pulled Molly down to cover him. Her breasts were crushed to his chest, and her legs trembled around him. Her mouth sought his in a long, hungry kiss. Meanwhile, Dash began to explore her curves. His fingertips felt like feathers, teasing gently but insistently.

He rolled her over onto her back on the carpet and began to ravage her neck with kisses. The rasp of his five-o'clock shadow was just as arousing on her skin as his mouth.

Learning, experimenting, reveling in the long-awaited moment, they wrestled on the floor for minutes or hours—Molly lost all track of anything outside the cushioned world they had created—until at last they were sitting with legs entangled in the bathroom doorway, breathing as if they'd run a marathon. Dash reached around, then turned the hot water lever on the tub.

"Come on," he whispered. "I want to see you in lots of bubbles, just the way I imagined."

Molly sat up on her knees and reached for the levers to close the drain and adjust the water temperature. As the steam rose up, Dash knelt behind her, wrapping his arms around Molly so he could caress her breasts while kissing the back of her neck. His erotic nibbles felt like tiny electrical charges on her skin as the steam enveloped them both.

"Lean forward," he instructed, then filled his hands with the weight of her breasts when she obeyed. When she raised her head, she saw her own reflection in the misty mirror, and as Dash lifted his head a moment later, their gazes met. Their expressions were astonishingly the same—clouded with passion, yet alight with a joyous glow.

"You're so beautiful," he said, continuing to caress her.

"You make me feel wonderful."

"I want to take you now."

"Not yet."

"You're ready. I can feel it." His fingers delved into her, but their gazes never wavered in the mirror. He said, "You're so responsive to me, Molly. Watch."

She watched the woman in the mirror as she grew more and more aroused under Dash's gentle touch. She saw the vulnerable expression in her eyes gradually replaced by a wonderfully wanton fierceness. In the circle of Dash's arms, she felt safe, exhilarated, cherished and . . . loved. The thought sent a rush of pleasure to all her nerve endings, and she cried out to him.

While she was still pulsing with pleasure, Dash turned Molly and clasped her against him, quieting her with his voice and gentle kisses. He whispered sweet, disjointed phrases in her ear.

"Molly, Molly, how have I managed so long without you? You're everything I need."

They slid into the tub then, warm flesh into soothing waters. The scented crystals were upended into the swirling water, and bubbles began to surge around them.

Molly eased into Dash's arms and sighed. "If this is how you kidnap someone, I'll be ready anytime."

"You're a model prisoner."

"I'll be your slave."

"I like that in a woman," he said on a laugh.

Molly kissed him long and warmly, parting her mouth and seeking the deepest recesses of his with her tongue.

"Mmm," he murmured, holding her head so he could control the intensity of the kiss. His hands slid into her hair. "Maybe I'll be your slave, too."

Molly smiled against his mouth. "I don't think you're the slave type."

"I didn't think I was the type for a lot of things," he said softly, punctuating his words with deft kisses. "Until you came along."

"I didn't do anything."

"Yes, you did. You're stubborn and demanding, and that's what it took to get me to recognize a few things."

"It got you talking. You're saying what's on your mind now instead of letting the rest of us guess."

He nodded, swiping the warm water from her face and following the dribbles with his lips. "Want to know what's on my mind now?"

"I think I know already."

"Touch me, Molly."

"Here?"

He bit off an exclamation when her caress became intimate. Then he swooped closer to kiss her, dragging her down into the bubbles with him. The sensual swish of water around her legs mingled with Dash's feathery caresses.

When she responded in kind, he groaned. "Slow down, Miss Molly, or this will be over any minute."

"You promised a whole night."

He seized her wrist and overpowered her easily, trapping Molly against the side of the tub and seeking her mouth once more. "I will. I'm going to make you weak."

She sighed. "I am already."

"Just wait. I want to make it good for you, Molly. Do you trust me?"

"Completely."

They played erotic games in the water, getting to know each other's desires. Molly ran her hands all over Dash's body, but gradually she knew he was too aroused to be teased. She sensed it in his tight words, the tautness of his muscles. He barely hung on to his passion, and the power that surged within him awed Molly. Soon she would be under his complete control. His intensity gave her pause, but she couldn't hold back. Her own passions ran rampant. The steam that rose up around them felt as if it billowed from their bodies, not just the hot water.

"Take me out of here," she begged at last. "Before I faint."

Dash pulled her from the tub and wrapped Molly in a thick white towel. Her skin felt hypersensitive as he dried her, but the tender expression in the back of his eyes gave her confidence. She watched him dry off, delighting in the opportunity to admire his powerful body and aching to make it her own.

He smoothed a damp tendril of hair away from her cheek, tilting her face up to his. "Better now? You're not going to faint?"

She felt her smile tremble. "For a different reason, maybe."

Dash grinned and carried her into the bedroom. Placing her on the bed, he then began to rummage in the tangle of their clothes for his jeans.

"What are you doing?"

"St. John gave me a condom. Remember? I've still got it somewhere."

Molly gulped and drew the bedclothes back with shaking hands. A moment later, Dash joined her, popping open the foil packet.

He was laughing. "This must be a first. A kid gives one of these gizmos to his old man, and here I am using it."

"You don't look old to me."

He waggled his brows mischievously. "You're about to enjoy the fruits of my experience, young lady."

"Can I help with that?"

Dash tossed it to her and slid into the bed. "Take your time, all right? I'll just lie back and enjoy it."

He didn't lie back, but he did seem to appreciate Molly's efforts. Soon they were tussling on the bed, nipping, laughing and spiraling higher into the stratosphere.

Dash had known she would be as exciting in bed as everywhere else in life. Molly's body was slender and strong, but extraordinarily sensitive, too. She quivered with tension, burned with desire. Her cheeks were whisker burned, and her mouth looked full and thoroughly kissed. A fine, beautiful flush rose up on the skin of her throat, heightening the blueness of her eyes.

And the expression in those eyes—naked, open, vulnerable—gave Dash an extraordinary feeling of satisfaction and pleasure as he caressed her. Then he watched them grow dark as he rolled above her and at last drove Molly deeply into the bed.

Though she was no virgin, he was glad to watch her discover her full powers as a woman beneath him. When he enfolded her in his arms and pressed into the center of her passion, she struggled at first and Dash relented, but she cried out, "No, don't stop."

"I don't want to hurt you."

"It feels wonderful," she gasped, then wrapped her legs around him and drew Dash even deeper inside her.

She met each slow, delicious wave by arching her back, thrusting her body against his. She met the increasing tempo with abandoned wildness.

She gave herself to him, wholly and eagerly. Dash took her into his heart. She belonged with him. She had forced her way in, and now he couldn't imagine living without her.

He was in love with her.

The thought drove him over the edge of sensibility. A storm overcame them, and Dash lost his head. Molly cried out again, passion beating against her relentlessly until at last she surrendered. Dash felt her convulse around him, and he pinned her fast to relish every heartbeat of her ecstasy.

Then his own body became a lightning bolt—dazzling and electric within the woman he'd come to love. Agonizing pleasure exploded in an incandescent moment, shaking Dash to his very core and wringing yet another joyous cry of release from Molly.

He was weak afterward, tired and yet wonderfully alive. In the aftermath, they clung to each other and spoke words that made no sense.

All Dash knew was that he'd found a woman unlike any other. But he couldn't find the way to tell her. It was easier to communicate with his body. He tried to love every inch of her, and along the way discovered more of her secrets. She liked his mouth here, his fingertips there. She loved to feel him deep within her. Her gaze was smoky and full of pleasure as she looked up into his face and pulled Dash down against her once more.

Their kisses grew sleepy in time.

"I'm so tired," she breathed in his ear.

So satisfied, Dash knew. "Sleep now," he whispered. "Sleep, my love."

But Molly had already drifted off and did not hear his endearment.

They both slept awhile, legs entangled and Molly's hair in ribbons around them. Dash woke up just a little while later, though he wasn't sure why. He sat up on one elbow.

There she was, dozing trustingly beside him. For a long time, he watched Molly breathe and the inviting way her mouth curled in her sleep. He was glad they'd left a light burning in the room while they made love, and he was even happier that neither one of them had had the strength to turn it off. He drank in every detail of Molly's naked body. Unable to restrain himself, he began to stroke her limbs very gently, hoping not to wake her. She was so beautiful, so full of fire. She sighed in her sleep, but didn't stir.

Perhaps she was enjoying an erotic dream, he thought, watching Molly relax beneath his slow caresses. He went on stimulating her in the gentlest way he could manage, brushing her skin as if with butterfly wings.

At last, he touched her warmest spot again. She caught her breath, but didn't wake. Dash was delighted to find she could respond even in a state of semiconsciousness. She moaned softly, but turned her face against the pillow, as if burrowing deeper into a delightful dream.

An idea caught him. Cautiously Dash eased Molly's legs apart. Her body seemed to arch against his fingertips, and when he replaced them with his lips, he felt Molly grow languidly aroused again.

But she didn't wake, just hovered in a state of drowsy sexual arousal. He was careful and gentle, doing exactly what he pleased with his tongue and sliding his fingers into her at just the right moment. When her inner fever broke this time, Molly released a long, passionate sigh. But she slept on, as if undisturbed by her secret lover.

Dash smiled and covered her with a sheet. She nestled against his chest, murmured something unintelligible and slept deeply. Dash held her in his arms and felt her heart beating against his.

A long time later, he remembered he should have told her about Dillon and the colt.

Molly woke early and found herself wrapped firmly in Dash's arms. He felt so strong and comforting against her—as if he could protect her from anything in the world. She loved waking up with him this way.

Shifting slightly, she didn't wake Dash, but felt his body stir, instinctively growing aroused against her. Unable to stop herself, Molly touched him and felt Dash grow even more firm against her hand. She caressed him softly and even slid out of his arms to kiss him there.

She wished she had the courage to wake him with a resounding climax. But a glance at the shadows underneath Dash's eyes told her that he hadn't slept well.

She stole out of bed, silently promising to come back in a couple of hours to give him a wake-up call he would remember for a long, long time.

Furtively she dressed in the bathroom and slipped outside the house as the dawn began to cast milky white rays across the landscape. She planned to see her other lover, Mashed Potato.

But he wasn't in his stall.

"What the hell—?"

Molly hurried out of the stallion barn where she'd found a place for Mashed Potato. She bumped into Julio in the lane.

"Julio, where is Mashed Potato?"

Julio looked like a man who wished he could be anywhere else on earth just then. "Uh, well—"

"He didn't run away, did he?"

"No, miss, he didn't run away."

"Then where is he?"

Julio swallowed hard. "Mr. Dillon took him this morning."

"What? Why?"

"He's over at the track, miss. They're going to run Mashed Potato with the other two-year-olds today."

Molly felt as if she'd been hit by a cannonball. "They're going to *run* him?"

"Yes, miss. A jockey's come up from Belmont Park, and he's going to try that colt himself."

"Are they *crazy?*"

She didn't give Julio a chance to answer. Molly ran across the lane to the place where her old pickup truck was parked. The keys were still in it, and she fired up the engine with a roar. In another minute, she was racing down the road toward the O'Donnelly practice track.

It wasn't hard to find Mashed Potato. He was the colt having a temper tantrum right in the middle of the track.

A jockey was on his back, slashing the colt's sides with a riding stick and cursing a blue streak. Dillon O'Donnelly himself held the colt's bridle, forcing Mashed Potato to dance in enraged circles while the other colts kept their distance. Seabiscuit was barking a blue streak himself and finally lunged in to seize Dillon by his trouser leg.

"Damn you!" Dillon shouted, releasing Mashed Potato to protect himself. "Somebody shoot this dog!"

"You shoot him," Molly cried, "and I'll turn the gun on you next!"

"What the hell are you doing here?"

Molly dragged her dog back from Dillon, saying, "Don't bite him, Biscuit, you might die of poisoning."

"Get off my track, young lady, before you get hurt!"

Free at last, Mashed Potato bucked twice and took off like greased lightning. His jockey had no choice but to cling to his back and go.

"Now see what you've done!" Dillon bellowed. "That colt's going to bulldoze anything in his path!"

"I hope you're squashed flat," Molly said furiously. "What the hell are you doing with him? That's my colt, damn you! Dash entrusted his training to me and I—"

"He's my colt now."

"Like hell!"

"I own him, and I train him."

"Dash will have something to say about that!"

"He already has." Dillon stuck his face down to Molly's and glared at her. "Last night, we agreed the colt was mine from now on."

"Last night?"

"You heard me. We decided you were too namby-pamby for a colt like Mashed Potato, so I added him to my string this morning. Your job is finished."

"You decided last night?" Molly repeated, trying desperately to make sense of what had happened. "You and Dash—?"

"We need a speed colt, not a children's pet," Dillon snapped. "So today he's out of your hands."

"But—"

"Collect your paycheck and go home," Dillon commanded. "I'm sure Dash will pay you the full amount."

Dillon spun away and hurried down the track to help catch Mashed Potato. Beside Molly, Seabiscuit gave a sad whine, and he nudged her hand.

Molly felt the burn of angry tears in her throat.

"Molly?"

Dash's shout caused her to turn around.

He climbed out of the Jeep and headed toward her rapidly, looking like a man who'd just rolled out of bed and realized he had a desperate mission to accomplish.

Molly shouted, "Just stay away from me, O'Donnelly!"

"I have to explain."

"Forget it."

He caught up with her just as Molly started to run for her truck. He grabbed her by the arm and spun her around to face him. He was out of breath, but not from exertion. Something like panic showed in his face. "Molly, let me explain what happened."

"You don't have to explain anything."

"I *had* to let Pop have the colt back. You know what's at stake. You were doing too good a job with him."

"And you did one hell of a job with me, didn't you?"

Dash's grip on her arm loosened. "Molly, don't."

"Don't what? Speak the truth?" she demanded in a rage. "You took me to bed last night to soften the blow, didn't you? I should have known something had changed! I was stupid to hope it was your damned cold heart!"

"Molly, what happened between you and me last night—"

"Was a mistake!"

"Like hell it was! It was wonderful, and you know it!"

The tears were hot in her throat and spilling down her face, and Molly couldn't stop them. "I thought it was wonderful, all right. I never guessed you did it to cover up what you and your son-of-a-bitch father cooked up."

"That's not what happened."

"You couldn't just *tell* me? You had to keep your damn secrets? My God, you're doing it again, aren't you?"

"Doing what?"

"Using a Pym to get what you want. You *used* me, Dash, just the way your father used mine."

"Are we back to that again? Molly, for God's sake—"

"There's nothing more important than a winner, is there? And you want one immediately. So you're taking Mashed Potato to the track when you *know* he's not ready yet."

"He *is* ready. Pop said—"

"What does your father know? Just how to take a promising young horse and break it down for a few quick races! He wants his money fast, and you can't see that he'll kill that colt in no time just the way he killed the filly he shared with my dad. Don't do it, Dash!''

He took a deep breath. "I have to," he said quietly. "I have to do what's best for the farm.''

Coldly Molly said, "No matter what happens to Mashed Potato? No matter what happens to us?''

"There's no need for you and me to be affected by what's going on here.''

"Are you *kidding*? Haven't you *learned* anything about me?''

"I've learned a lot. I've learned you're stubborn, for one thing—maybe too stubborn to put the past aside and make the future work. We could have a lot together, Molly. If you'd just forget about your father—''

"You want me to forget who I am," she said, flabbergasted.

"Of course not.''

"Yes, you do. You want me to roll over and do exactly what you ask, even though I know what's right.''

"Damn you, Molly—''

"Forget it," she said, snapping open the truck door. "Just forget you ever met me, O'Donnelly. You obviously never really knew me at all.''

"Molly—''

She didn't hear him after that. Her truck started with a spluttering roar, and she jammed it into gear. Seabiscuit had just enough time to jump in through the passenger window. Then Molly roared out of Dash O'Donnelly's life and headed for home.

Ten

___

Dash sent his children back to New York when their mother returned from her trip. Then he spent three weeks getting ready for the annual yearling sales. He talked with potential buyers and wooed them with fancy dinners. He worked numbers with his bankers. He spent hours at the track.

All in hopes of forgetting about Molly Pym.

Damn her.

She couldn't read what was in his heart? She couldn't figure out the truth for herself? Couldn't she see he'd never meant to lie to her or steal her precious colt away?

Why did she have to *hear the words?* Why couldn't she just believe him? Damn her, damn her, damn her.

Well, he'd just forget about her. A woman who was too demanding was a woman who wasn't worth having.

* * *

Molly left the state and drove to Florida.

She made arrangements with her boarders and sent their horses to other barns, then cashed the forty-five-hundred-dollar check that came in the mail from O'Donnelly Farms with *no note, damn him,* and got into her truck and drove south.

Her truck broke down in South Carolina, where a garage mechanic declared it dead on arrival.

She rented a car, since the bus wouldn't accept Seabiscuit, and arrived at her mother's place around four in the afternoon.

"Molly!" Her mother looked frightened when she opened the door. "What on earth are you doing here?"

Molly was prepared to soothe her mother and tell her everything was all right, but it wasn't, so she burst into tears and was hastily ushered into the house for tea and pecan cookies at the kitchen table.

Her mother's friend Dolores fussed over the teapot, while Margaret Pym anxiously tried to stanch Molly's tears.

"Honey, what's wrong? Is it the farm? Did it burn? Did you have an accident? Tell me, please!"

It was several minutes before Molly could choke out her story, and just a few more minutes after that before Margaret figured out things didn't involve life or death. She pressed a cup into Molly's hands and talked about the weather until Molly pulled herself together and admitted there was a man behind it all.

"I know I've flown off the handle," she admitted to her mother. "But he's such a—a—oh, I don't know."

Margaret and Dolores nodded sympathetically.
"Men are like that," said Dolores. "They chew up
your heart and spit it out so they can go play golf
whenever they feel like it."

"Golf?"

"My Charlie played golf all the time. Had a heart
attack on the VFW course and died before the ambu-
lance got there. Serves him right, I say!"

Margaret rolled her eyes. "I'm sure Molly just needs
time to calm down while her young man gets his act
together."

Molly shook her head. "He'll never get his act together, Mom. It's too hard for him. He'd rather cruise
through life all alone than make the effort to—to—"

"There, there, Molly. You cry all you like." Margaret patted her shoulders. "Some time in the sunshine will be just the ticket for you. Why, we'll drive
out to the track tomorrow, too. Won't that be fun?
And you can sit on the beach, and go swimming...."

Molly liked the sound of her mother's prescription.
She sniffed and lifted her chin and determined to get
her life back to normal.

The beach was hot and baked her skin to a golden
tan in a matter of a few days. The track was fun, and
Molly helped her mother and Dolores win eighty dollars at the betting windows the first time. They ate
fried fish and cole slaw, drank iced tea by the gallon
and played endless card games—some of which Molly
didn't understand and suspected Dolores made up just
so she could win the penny pots. On the hot after-
noons, the older women watched soap operas on television and took naps. All day long, Seabiscuit slept on
the linoleum floor, panting in the heat and keeping a

watchful eye on Molly in case she tried to leave without him.

They stayed for a week. And then another week. And pretty soon the month of July was flitting by. Molly settled into life at the apartment complex, but she felt restless. She didn't sleep at night, and instead tossed and mumbled and tried not to dream.

But Dash kept reappearing. Saying nothing, but making her feel like a woman.

On a Wednesday afternoon, with *The Young and the Restless* coming to a slow climax, Molly heard her mother's doorbell ring, and since both of the other women were asleep in their easy chairs, she said, "I'll get it."

The last person she expected to see standing there was Dillon O'Donnelly.

"So here you are," he said, glaring at her in the bright Florida sunlight.

Molly could only stare.

"I've come looking for you," he growled.

"How did you know where to look?"

He was walking with a cane, and rapped it impatiently against the bottom of his shoe. "We're racing some three-year-olds at the track. Julio saw you by chance."

"Julio?" *Where's Dash?* Molly wanted to ask.

Dillon pointed with his cane. "He's down in the car right now. Says he's afraid to come up here."

"Smart guy, Julio." She eyed Dillon warily. "What happened to you?"

He looked grouchy. "The cane, you mean? Well, what do you expect? That damned colt of yours kicked me. I'll probably have to have my knee replaced this winter."

There were lots of wisecracks Molly could have made just then—like what other body parts he ought to have replaced at the same time. But she said, "He's not my colt."

"No, that's true," Dillon agreed. "But he needs you."

Molly wasn't sure she'd heard right. But to spare her mother from seeing Dillon, she stepped outside and closed the apartment door behind her. Then she strolled across the balcony, turned and leaned against the rail to face the old man.

"You hear what I said?" Dillon demanded. "The colt needs you."

"I heard you the first time. I'm just trying to figure out why you came all this way to tell me."

Dillon nodded. "Okay, it looks suspicious, I know. I tried to get Dash to find you and get you back, but he wouldn't do it." In a mutter probably not meant to be heard, he added, "Dash isn't really speaking to me these days, as a matter of fact."

Molly tried not to look too interested. "Oh?"

"He's mad at me. Says I'm part of the problem. I can't see it, myself, but he's—well, he's a smart enough fellow, I suppose. He'd like you to come back and help us with our colt, but he won't do it unless I promise to keep my nose out of it. I can't do that, can I?"

She folded her arms over her chest. "You poke your nose just about any place you like, I guess."

Dillon puffed up his cheeks, then blew out an impatient breath. "Look, let's stop beating around the bush, shall we? I'm here with my hat in my hand, girl. The least you can do is meet me halfway. We need you."

Molly waited.

"We need you because that colt is still too wild to race. But we've entered him in the Hopeful. It's this Saturday."

Molly knew all about the Hopeful. It was a race for promising two-year-olds and was used as one of the preliminary races for the Kentucky Derby and the Triple Crown in the spring. A colt that made a good showing in the Hopeful was a colt to watch next year.

She understood what it would mean to Dash to have a colt run in the Hopeful.

"You were a fool to enter him."

"Maybe so, but it's done. I hate to scratch him now."

"So?" she asked.

Dillon glared at her. "You're gonna make me say it, aren't you?"

"Yep."

"All right," he declared. "I want you to get on the plane with me and come back to Saratoga. You help me with the colt, and maybe he'll be able to run on Saturday. Of course, maybe he'll turn out to be a dud—"

"He won't."

"Or maybe he'll be a winner."

"That's what you like, isn't it? Just winners."

"You got something against winners?'"

Molly felt tired—too tired to explain human ethics to a man who was too old to learn. "No," she said wearily. "I just can't be as ruthless as you."

He nodded. "You're holding your pop against me. Well, maybe I was wrong back then. Maybe I should have held on to that filly and let him work with her. But I didn't, and—and that's my mistake. But I didn't kill him, you know. It was his bad luck to die at the wrong time.''

"You want me to kiss and forget?"

"Hell, no," Dillon snapped. "You can hate me until your grave—or my grave, whichever comes first— but you can stop letting your feelings about me mess things up between you and my son."

Molly stiffened. "What do you know about that?"

"All I want to know," Dillon said, putting an end to that subject. "Well, what's your answer? You coming?"

"I don't have to help you."

"No, but turning your back on me is turning your back on Dash, and you don't want to do that, do you?"

"N-no."

"Then come on. Get your gear. We're flying back this afternoon."

"Listen," Molly said. "I don't want to see Dash, all right?"

Dillon fixed her with a fierce look. "Why not?"

"That's my business. I'm not going back to your house, and I won't hang around your farm. I'll help with your colt because he's going to be great, and I don't want you ruining him. But that's it. I go no further. I've got my reasons, and they're not your concern. Got it?"

"I don't give a flying fig about your reasons, girl. I just want you at the track on Saturday."

Walking into the Saratoga Season was like stepping back in time. The whole town was festooned in decorations—the flower kind and the human kind. The candy shops and sidewalk cafés overflowed with rich and famous race-goers. The newspapers were full of excitement. The local hotels and charming bed-and-breakfast inns were overflowing with tourists eager to watch the annual horse races at the beautiful Saratoga racetrack.

The old wooden grandstand and clubhouse were lovely—crowded with well-dressed people and lavishly draped in red-and-white awnings. Ladies wore huge picture hats, and the men sported straw boaters. The few children wandering the lushly landscaped grounds were equally well dressed and well behaved.

But Molly avoided the public areas of the park. For three days, she arrived by the back entrance and found the stable where the O'Donnelly horses were being housed for the race day.

The back alleys of racetracks were a second home to Molly Pym. She'd been sitting on hay bales shooting the breeze with all manner of stable hands, stakes trainers and railbirds since she'd been old enough to talk.

"Hey, Molly! What you been doing, girl?"

"Is that Molly Pym? Get over here, young lady! Let me have a look at you! Why, she's pretty as a picture, ain't she, Blackie?"

"Why, Molly, I heard you're still trying to make a go of that farm your daddy bought back in '49. Didn't you learn nothing from all those years of Paddy breaking his back?"

Molly waved to everyone and shook hands with a few rough old cobs. For the first time in many weeks, she felt like breathing again. She'd been welcomed home by her surrogate family—a mismatched and sometimes illiterate bunch of characters, perhaps, but family just the same.

She was glad to see Mashed Potato, and he was just as delighted to see her again, too. She fed him a sprig of mint and whispered sweet nothings in his ear while he nibbled his treat and then rubbed his face all over her shirt.

She breezed him herself on Thursday and Friday morning, refusing to allow anyone near the colt until he was calm and centered once again. He responded to her patience, but in her opinion he was still too untamed to race. He was more interested in fighting with the other colts galloping on the track than running himself. She recommended that he be scratched from the Hopeful.

But Dillon refused to listen.

On Saturday, amid the excitement of race day, Molly saddled him herself in the O'Donnelly colors of emerald green and white, then led the colt out into the paddock with the other colts slated to run in the Hopeful.

The Saratoga paddock was one of the most beautiful in the country, with shade trees, beautiful fences to hold back the crowds, and the red-and-white Saratoga banners fluttering in the breeze. Mashed Potato pricked his ears and danced in circles to get a good look at the crowd. He was excited, and no amount of soothing could settle him down. Within minutes, he was lathered with sweat and yanking Molly's arm out of its socket.

"This is crazy," she said to Dillon when he arrived to boost the jockey into Mashed Potato's saddle. "Somebody's going to get killed."

"Get out of the way, girl, if you're too scared."

"I'm not scared! Give me that!" She snatched back the lead rein and said, "I'll take him onto the track myself."

Dillon nodded. "We'll have the pony waiting for you." He turned away, hesitated, then faced her again. Gruffly he said, "There's just one thing I want to tell you before the race."

"Whatever it is, it's too late now."

"Maybe not. With that chip you carry on your shoulder, I'm not sure you'll ever amount to anything," Dillon said. "But if you'd cool down once in a while, you'd be a hard act to beat."

Molly stared at him. "Why are you saying this now?"

"The time's not important. You could be great, just like your pop. But you've got a few things to learn, still. No matter what happens today, you get yourself a decent job, working for a real trainer."

"I don't sweep out stables, you know."

"You won't have to start at the bottom."

"Women always have to prove themselves."

"Not you," Dillon said, with surprising generosity. "You're going places in this business, young lady—unless you blow it out of pride. That's all I'm going to say."

It was enough. He walked away and didn't look back.

An employee of the stable always led the racehorse onto the track, despite the fact that a jockey was in the saddle. Perched on the tiny saddle with the stirrups run up high, however, it was hard to control a plunging animal, so a stable hand on another horse—called a pony by tradition—tried to keep the racehorse from getting out of hand. Molly led Mashed Potato and his jockey, old pro Willy Bartman, pumped her for ideas about the coming race.

"What can you tell me, Molly?" Willy asked over the dull roar of the mob that surged around the paddock where they circled with the other entrants.

"Didn't Dillon give you your instructions?"

"Yeah," Willy said with a laugh. "Just stay on his back and see what happens. I hate instructions like that, Molly. They make me nervous."

"Just hold on to him as long as you can," Molly advised. "I'm not sure what he'll do in the lead. Keep him in the pack until the last minute. I think you'll still have a lot of horse under you when the time comes."

"Okay," Willy said, snapping the strap on his helmet and gathering up the reins.

Molly mounted the piebald horse from O'Donnelly Farms.

"Molly! Molly! Hey, Molly!"

Hearing her name shouted from the crowd, Molly looked around and spied a threesome of handsomely dressed young people, all jumping up and down, looking excited. "Hey, Molly! It's us!"

Montgomery, Nikki and St. John. They were waving frantically, all smiles. "Good luck!" they screamed. "See you in the winner's circle!"

Molly saw immediately that Dash was not with the kids. She waved to them, then got down to business.

Mashed Potato didn't like to be led, but Molly insisted he behave himself. She reined her own mount close to him and kept a firm hand on the lead rein. Following the other colts, they trooped across the lawn and through the eerily echoing tunnel beneath the grandstand. Once through, they stepped into the sunshine and were deafened by the blasting loudspeaker and the roar of the crowd. Mashed Potato's eyes blazed. He tried to bolt, feeling the track under his hooves and smelling speed on the wind. Molly and Willy fought together to keep him under control.

Molly concentrated on the colt and tuned out the rest of the world. It was a hard battle, but they managed to get him as far as the starting gate without hurting himself or anyone else. When he heard the bugle for the first time, he reared and pawed the air.

When he saw the gate, though, Mashed Potato lunged toward it with excitement, yanking the lead rein through Molly's hand so hard it cut into her flesh. She yelped, but hung on until one of the starters jumped forward to take the colt into the starting gate.

"Wish me luck," Willy called to her as they led him into the gate.

"Good luck," Molly called, then added softly, "You'll need it."

Her last glimpse of Mashed Potato was the shining darkness of his rump as he disappeared into the gate.

Molly turned her pony and rode back to the tunnel. Like the other leaders, she jumped off her mount and elbowed her way up onto the fence crowded with railbirds to watch the race.

It was a hell of a race, she was told later. And the television reruns were unbelievable.

All Molly saw was a fast break from the gate—all colts except Mashed Potato plunging out simultaneously and running for the first turn. Mashed Potato broke badly, plunged toward the rail and stumbled before collecting his courage and launching himself after the pack with the speed of a demon.

The two-year-old colts flashed past the grandstand in a tight pack—with Mashed Potato trailing behind.

Molly's eyes stung as she watched her love driving for the other colts with all his strength. And he was catching up! Willy sat still and let him run. As the rest of the colts rounded the first turn, Mashed Potato had caught their tails and nosed his way into the bunch.

As the colts hit the backstretch and started the long run there, Mashed Potato fought his way through the pack. The cheering thousands jammed into the grandstand suddenly jumped to their feet as the colts raced for the far turn.

"Holy cow!" someone shouted in Molly's ear. "Is that your colt? Man, he's— *Holy cow!*"

Then everybody went berserk, screaming, churning. Molly grabbed for the fence, her heart pounding, but in the next instant somebody hit her with his elbow and Molly was jostled off the fence. She fell into a mass of people, who were all screaming and jumping up and down. She clawed her way up, but couldn't see the track, couldn't see what was happening. The roar around her was like a freight train.

She only heard the shouted words of the track announcer who called, "It's Passion by a neck, Nantucket second and Hot Money in third...."

Mashed Potato's name was not among the winners.

She turned away from the track and grabbed the reins of her pony. There was no use fighting the crowd to get to Mashed Potato now. Willy and one of the track helpers would get him back to the stable. Molly led her pony through the tunnel, hurrying to get to the stall in time to cool down Mashed Potato and make sure he was all right.

Bedlam in the stables. Molly ducked out of the way as the next group of colts swept by for their race, then she was greeted by a hysterical pack of O'Donnelly employees.

"He didn't win," she kept saying as they jumped up and down like monkeys and yelled complete nonsense at her. "He didn't win."

They didn't seem to understand and rushed past her, heading for the track.

Mashed Potato didn't come back. Five minutes, ten minutes passed. Molly began to worry.

At last, he came, surrounded by stable hands, Dillon, the three children—and Dash, leading the colt by his reins.

"You idiot" were Dash's first words. "Where have you been?"

"Where have *you* been? What happened?"

"He *won,* Molly."

"But—but—I didn't hear his name."

Montgomery leapt forward, hugging her. "Because we changed it! Dad, she didn't know his new name!"

"What? What new name?"

"Pym's Passion," Dash said, letting go of Mashed Potato and pulling Molly into his arms. "We thought you'd approve."

Eleven

Dash was bitterly disappointed.

He said, "The *New York Times* didn't print a picture of him."

Molly laughed and made room in the bed for Dash and all his newspapers. She plumped up the pillows, and he climbed in beside her, strewing all but the sports pages all over the bedroom floor. She said, "But they're good stories about Mashed Potato, right?"

"Pym's Passion," Dash corrected, putting one arm around Molly's bare shoulders and pulling her close so they could read the article together. "Sure, they're all good stories, just like they told us last night. But I was hoping they'd use a photograph."

"Dash, they're calling him the favorite for the Derby—and he's just run his first race!"

"But a hell of a race," Dash said dreamily. "I wish you could have seen it."

"The evening-news version was good enough." Molly snuggled down and sighed. "Oh, Dash, I hope we're not getting overconfident. A lot could happen between now and next spring."

Dash tossed the newspaper aside and gathered Molly into his arms again. "A lot *could* happen," he said softly. "But it's all going to be good."

She gazed into his face and ran one finger down the line of his cheek. "I missed you," she murmured.

"I nearly went crazy after you left."

"I was angry. I thought you'd conspired with your father against me."

"I hope you know how wrong you were. It was my ignorance about this business that led me to believe we were doing the right thing by racing Passion as soon as we did. We needed a break, Molly. It never occurred to me we were risking his future."

"I shouldn't have gotten so mad. I should have stayed and talked about it."

He smiled sadly. "Maybe being around me got you out of the habit of talking. I'm not much of a communicator."

"You'll learn," she promised, pressing a heartfelt kiss on his cheek. Another followed, then a third, and pretty soon she was kissing his mouth and savoring the sensations that swept over them both.

When they parted, Dash said, "You know what I hated most? You leaving."

"I'm sorry."

He shook his head. "It taught me a lesson, though. I realized I'd been doing it since I was St. John's age. When things got too tough for me, I packed my bags and left. I never knew how hard that must have been on the people I loved—until you did it to me."

"Oh, Dash—"

"No, don't apologize. It must have nearly killed my father when I first ran away. But he didn't know how to come after me, so it became a habit. When things didn't work out with my ex-wife, I took off again. She found life easier without me, so she let me go, too."

"I'm glad you came after me, Dash."

Molly blushed, remembering how she'd lost her cool yesterday, after the race and the crush of excitement afterward. She'd tried to slip away, reassured that Mashed Potato—or Pym's Passion—had been properly taken care of. She hadn't wanted her reunion with Dash to take place in public.

But he'd found her sliding out of the barn and heading for home and had captured her.

"If you won't stand here and talk to me," he'd said, "I'll have to kidnap you."

"You wouldn't!"

But he had. Dash had bundled Molly into his convertible and driven all the way to O'Donnelly Farms without stopping, in case she decided to jump out of the car at the first opportunity. It was a foolish kind of pride that had made her so furious.

That night, they'd fought a terrible battle, but somehow things had ended up in the bedroom. They'd made love fiercely and explosively. Then spent the rest of the night talking in circles about things that didn't seem to matter—just getting to know each other. In the morning, Molly woke up feeling much differently about Dash O'Donnelly.

"I hope," he said, kissing her once more, "that I'll never have to come after you again."

"I don't think so."

"Can I make you promise?"

Thinking of the future, Molly balked. If Dillon was right, maybe she'd better go looking for a real job with a top-notch trainer. Maybe Dash had finally found a home for himself, but she still had a long way to go.

Dash saw her expression. "Molly," he said, voice soft but urgent. "Tell me you'll stay here."

"Dash—"

"I need you," he said. "I love you."

The words, when they finally came, shook Molly deeply. Dash's gaze was steady, though, and she knew he meant what he said. "Oh, Dash, I love you, too. But things are so messy for me right now—"

"They don't have to be. Let me help."

"I have to do some things on my own."

"Please," he said. "I know it's hard to give up on your father's farm. But I want you here. We could be good together, Molly. I want to marry you."

"Marry me?"

"It's the only way," he said. "Marry me and work here at O'Donnelly Farms. My father won't be physically able to run things this winter, and we'll need to get Pym's Passion ready for the Triple Crown—"

"But you've got dozens of horses to train—"

"And I can't do it myself. I have no experience."

"I don't have enough. I'm just getting started."

"You can keep us on track, though. We need you, Molly. I need you more than anything. I love you. Marry me."

His words weren't enough, Dash decided. He wasn't saying them right. So he began to use the methods he knew could weaken Molly into accepting. He kissed her lips, her forehead, her nose, her earlobes. He nibbled her throat and found her nipples with his tongue.

"Dash—" she breathed, lacing her fingers into his hair.

"I love you," he said against her skin.

"Oh, Dash."

She arched against him erotically. Her voice trembled and her skin seemed to shiver beneath his caresses. He trailed his lips all over her body and found the sweetest spot again, teasing it until she writhed in his arms. In time, Dash sought her lips again and relished the way she opened herself to him. Pinning her to the bed once more, he took her gently.

She wrapped her arms around his neck and murmured nonsense in his ear. He loved the sounds of pleasure that purred in the back of her throat. He adored her red hair, strong will and sassy tongue. He cherished the abandon with which she gave herself to him.

"Marry me," he urged, as she balanced on the edge of complete pleasure.

"Yes," she breathed. "Oh, yes, yes, yes."

They plunged into that wonderful abyss of ecstasy together.

Later, still languishing in the pleasure of each other's eyes, Molly said, "I love you, Dash."

"Good Golly," he replied, "I love you, too, Miss Molly."

*   *   *   *   *

COMING NEXT MONTH

MIKE'S BABY
Mary Lynn Baxter

Joanna Nash hated exercise and hated the thought of a
personal trainer even more. But Mike McCoy had a very
masterful touch and was keen to get personal with
Joanna...

MAYBE NO, MAYBE YES
Cait London

Sloan Raventhrall needed help when he caught the flu from
his visiting niece. He called in co-worker Melanie
Inganforde, but her services came with a hefty price
attached!

DEVIL OR ANGEL
Audra Adams

Bitter from a fifteen-year-old betrayal, Devon Taylor
returned to his home town to seek revenge. But Brooke
Wallace was more than the sweet angel he had left
behind...

Silhouette Desire

COMING NEXT MONTH

A FLEETING MOMENT
Carla Cassidy

Cliff Marchelli was asking to spend his nights at her
apartment and Edie knew she ought to say yes. After all,
Cliff was a cop wanting to set up a stakeout, but he was
too sexy to ignore night after night...

THE COWBOY AND THE PRINCESS
Joan Johnston

Another novel about the Whitelaws of Texas.

Faron Whitelaw was off to claim an inheritance from a
father he'd never known, but a beautiful woman in a
sunlit meadow distracted him. How could he have
guessed that he was making love to his step-mother?

QUICKSAND
Jennifer Greene

Man of the Month Cooper Maitland decided that it was
time he stopped working so hard, got to know his
teenage daughter and settled down in his old home town.
But Priss Neilson, his neighbour, was downright
unsettling!